burned

Ellen Hopkins

Margaret K. McElderry Books
New York   London   Toronto   Sydney

This book is dedicated to my exceptional editor and support system, Julia Richardson. With special thanks to Kathleen Jones, who found the courage to forge her own path, and without whose help this book would not have been as accurate a glimpse of a young woman struggling with her religion.

Margaret K. McElderry Books
An imprint of Simon & Schuster Children's Publishing Division
1230 Avenue of the Americas, New York, NY 10020
Copyright © 2006 by Ellen Hopkins
All rights reserved, including the right of reproduction in whole or in part in any form.
Also available in a Margaret K. McElderry Books hardcover edition.
Designed by Sammy Yuen Jr.
The text of this book was set in Caledonia.
Manufactured in the United States of America
First Simon Pulse edition October 2007
10
The Library of Congress has cataloged the hardcover edition as follows:
Hopkins, Ellen.
p. cm.
Summary: Seventeen-year-old Pattyn, the eldest daughter in a large Mormon family, is sent to her aunt's Nevada ranch for the summer, where she temporarily escapes her alcoholic, abusive father and finds love and acceptance, only to lose everything when she returns home.
ISBN-13: 978-1-4169-0354-3 (hc)
ISBN-10: 1-4169-0354-2 (hc)
[1. Family problems—Fiction. 2. Mormons—Fiction. 3. Alcoholism—Fiction.
4. Identity—Fiction. 5. Sex—Fiction. 6. Aunts—Fiction. 7. Nevada—Fiction.] I. Title.
PZ7.H7747Bu 2006
[Fic]—dc22   2005032461
ISBN-13: 978-1-4169-0355-0 (pbk)
ISBN-10: 1-4169-0355-0 (pbk)

Did You Ever

When you were little, endure
your parents' warnings, then wait
for them to leave the room,
pry loose protective covers
and consider inserting some metal
object into an electrical outlet?

        Did you wonder if for once
        you might light up the room?

When you were big enough
to cross the street on your own,
did you ever wait for a signal,
hear the frenzied approach
of a fire truck and feel like
stepping out in front of it?

        Did you wonder just how far
        that rocket ride might take you?

When you were almost grown,
did you ever sit in a bubble bath,
perspiration pooling,
notice a blow-dryer plugged
in within easy reach, and think
about dropping it into the water?

                Did you wonder if the expected
                rush might somehow fail you?

And now, do you ever dangle
your toes over the precipice,
dare the cliff to crumble,
defy the frozen deity to suffer
the sun, thaw feather and bone,
take wing to fly you home?

                I, Pattyn Scarlet Von Stratten, do.

I'm Not Exactly Sure

When I began to feel that way.
      Maybe a little piece of me
always has. It's hard to remember.

But I do know things really
      began to spin out of control
after my first sex dream.

As sex dreams go, there wasn't
      much sex, just a collage
of very hot kisses, and Justin Proud's

hands, exploring every inch
      of my body, at my fervent
invitation. As a stalwart Mormon

high school junior, drilled
      ceaselessly about the dire
catastrophe awaiting those

who harbored impure thoughts,
      I had never kissed a boy,
had never even considered

that I might enjoy such
      an unclean thing, until
literature opened my eyes.

See, the Library

was my sanctuary. — Then I started high
Through middle — school, where the
school, librarians — not-so-bookish
were like guardian — librarian was half
angels. Spinsterish — angel, half she-devil,
guardian angels, — so sayeth the rumor
with graying hair — mill. I hardly cared.
and beady eyes, — Ms. Rose was all
magnified through — I could hope I might
reading glasses, — one day be: aspen
and always ready — physique, new penny
to recommend new — hair, aurora green
literary windows — eyes, and hands that
to gaze through. — could speak. She
A. A. Milne. Beatrix — walked on air. Ms.
Potter. Lewis — Rose shuttered old
Carroll. Kenneth — windows, opened
Grahame. E. B. — portals undreamed of.
White. Beverly — And just beyond,
Cleary. Eve Bunting. — what fantastic worlds!

I Met Her My Freshman Year

All wide-eyed and dim about starting high school,
a big new school, with polished hallways
and hulking lockers and doors that led
who-knew-where?

A scary new school, filled with towering
teachers and snickering students,
impossible schedules, tough expectations,
and endless possibilities.

The library, with its paper perfume,
whispered queries, and copy
machine shuffles, was the only familiar
place on the entire campus.

> And there was Ms. Rose.
> *How can I help you?*

Fresh off a fling with C. S.
Lewis and Madeleine L'Engle,
hungry for travel far from home,
I whispered, "Fantasy, please."

> She smiled. *Follow me.*
> *I know just where to take you.*

I shadowed her to Tolkien's
Middle-earth and Rowling's
School of Witchcraft and Wizardry,
places no upstanding Mormon should go.
                    When you finish those,
                    I'd be happy to show you more.

Fantasy Segued into Darker Dimensions

And authors who used three whole names:
Vivian Vande Velde, Annette Curtis Klause.
Mary Downing Hahn.

By my sophomore year, I was deep
into adult horror—King, Koontz, Rice.

> *You must try classic horror,*
> insisted Ms. Rose.

Poe, Wells, Stoker. Stevenson. Shelley.

> *There's more to life than monsters.*
> *You'll love these authors:*

Burroughs. Dickens. Kipling. London.
Bradbury. Chaucer. Henry David Thoreau.

> *And these:*

Jane Austen. Arthur Miller. Charlotte Brontë.
F. Scott Fitzgerald. J. D. Salinger.

By my junior year, I devoured increasingly
adult fare. Most, I hid under my dresser:

D. H. Lawrence. Truman Capote.
Ken Kesey. Jean Auel.
Mary Higgins Clark. Danielle Steel.

I Began

To view the world at large
through borrowed eyes,
eyes more like those
I wanted to own.

                              Hopeful.

I began
to see that it was more than
okay—it was, in some circles,
expected—to question my
little piece of the planet.

                              Empowered.

I began
to understand that I could
stretch if I wanted to, explore
if I dared, escape
if I just put one foot
in front of the other.

                              Enlightened.

I began
to realize that escape
might offer the only real
hope of freedom from my
supposed God-given roles—
wife and mother of as many
babies as my body could bear.

Emboldened.

I Also Began to Journal

Okay, one of the things expected of Latter-
Day Saints is keeping a journal.

But I'd always considered it just another
"supposed to," one not to worry much about.

Besides, what would I write in a book
everyone was allowed to read?

Some splendid nonfiction chronicle
about sharing a three-bedroom house

with six younger sisters, most of whom
I'd been required to diaper?

Some suspend-your-disbelief fiction
about how picture-perfect life was at home,

forget the whole dysfunctional truth
about Dad's alcohol-fueled tirades?

Some brilliant manifesto about how God
whispered sweet insights into my ear,

higher truths that I would hold on to forever,
once I'd shared them through testimony?

Or maybe they wanted trashy confessions—
Daydreams Designed by Satan.

Whatever. I'd never written but a few
words in my mandated diary.

Maybe it was the rebel in me.
Or maybe it was just the lazy in me.

But faithfully penning a journal
was the furthest thing from my mind.

Ms. Rose Had Other Ideas

One day I brought a stack of books,
most of them banned in decent LDS
households, to the checkout counter.

> Ms. Rose looked up and smiled.
> *You are quite the reader, Pattyn.*
> *You'll be a writer one day, I'll venture.*

I shook my head. "Not me.
Who'd want to read anything
I have to say?"

> She smiled. *How about you?*
> *Why don't you start*
> *with a journal?*

So I gave her the whole
lowdown about why journaling
was not my thing.

> *A very good reason to keep*
> *a journal just for you. One*
> *you don't have to write in.*

A day or two later, she gave
me one—plump, thin-lined,
with a plain denim cover.

Decorate it with your words,
she said. *And don't be afraid*
of what goes inside.

I Wasn't Sure What She Meant

Until I opened the stiff-paged volume
and started to write.

At first, rather ordinary fare
garnished the lines.

*Feb. 6. Good day at school. Got an A
on my history paper.*

*Feb. 9. Roberta has strep throat. Great!
Now we'll all get it.*

But as the year progressed, I began
to feel I was living in a stranger's body.

*Mar. 15. Justin Proud smiled at me today.
I can't believe it! And I can't believe
how it made me feel. Kind of tingly all over,
like I had an itch I didn't want to scratch.
An itch you-know-where.*

*Mar. 17. I dreamed about Justin last night.
Dreamed he kissed me, and I kissed him back,
and I let him touch me all over my body*

and I woke up all hot and blushing.
Blushing! Like I'd done something wrong.
Can a dream be wrong?
Aren't dreams God's way
of telling you things?

Justin Proud

Was one of the designated
"hot bods" on campus.
        No surprise all the girls
hotly pursued that bod.

        The only surprise was my
subconscious interest.
        I mean, he was anything
but a good Mormon boy.

        And I, allegedly being
a good Mormon girl,
        was supposed to keep
my feminine thoughts pure.

        Easy enough, while struggling
with stacks of books,
        piles of paper, and mounds
of adolescent angst.

        Easy enough, while chasing
after a herd of siblings,
        each the product of lustful,
if legally married, behavior.

Easy enough, while watching
other girls pant after him.
But just how do you maintain
pure thoughts when you dream?

I Suppose That's the Kind of Thing

Some girls could ask their moms.
    But Mom and I didn't talk
        a whole lot about what
            makes the world go round.

Conversation tended to run
    toward who'd wash the dishes,
        who'd dust and vacuum,
            who'd change the diapers.

In a house with seven kids,
    the oldest always seemed to draw
        diaper duty. Mom worked real
            hard to avoid Luvs. In fact,

that's the hardest she ever
    worked at anything. Am I saying
        my mom was lazy? I guess I am.
            As more of us girls went off

to school each day, the house
    got dirtier and dirtier. If we
        wanted clean clothes,
            we loaded the washer.

If we wanted clean dishes,
        we had to clear the sink.
                Mom watched a lot of TV.
                        She didn't have a job, of course.

Dad wouldn't hear of it, which
        made Mom extremely happy.
                I think she saw her profession as
                        populating the world with girls.

Seven Girls

That's all Mom ever
managed to give Dad.
He named every one after
a famous general, always
planning on a son.

A son, to replace the two
his first wife had given him,
the two he'd lost.

Janice, I heard him tell Mom
more than once, *if you don't
pop out a boy next time,
I'm getting my money back on you.*

But she carried no
money-back guarantee.
And the baby girls
just kept coming.

In reverse order: Georgia
(another nod to General
George Patton, my namesake);
Roberta (Robert E. Lee);
Davie (Jefferson D.);

Teddie (Roosevelt);
Ulyssa (S. Grant);
Jackie (Pershing).
Oh yes, and me.
No nicknames,
no shortcuts,
use every syllable,
every letter,
because
there would
be no "half-ass"
in Dad's house.

It's disturbing, I know.
But Dad was Dad
so Mom went along.

One Time, One Day

between Davie
I asked my mom
kept on having

and Roberta,
why she persisted,
baby after baby.

She looked

at me, at a spot
blinking like I had
crazy. She paused

between my eyes,
suddenly fallen
before answering

as if

to confide would
She drew a deep
the chair. I touched

legitimize my fears.
breath, leaned against
her hand and I thought

she might

cry. Instead she put
Pattyn, she said,
I decided if it was

baby Davie in my arms.
it's a woman's role.
my role, I'd rather

disappear.

In My View, Having Babies

was supposed to be
something

        beautiful,

not a duty.
Something

        incredible,

not role-playing.
Bringing

        new life

into this dying
world,

        promising hope

for a saner
tomorrow.

        As I saw it,

any expectation
of sanity rested

        in a woman's womb.

God should have
given Eve

        another chance.

Instead, He turned
her away, no way

        to make the world better.

Regardless

Barring blizzards
      or bouts of projectile vomiting,
I attended Sunday services

      every week, and that week
was no exception. Three solid
      hours of crying babies

and uninspired testimony,
      all orchestrated by bishops,
presidents, prophets, and priests,

      each bearing a masculine
moniker, specialized "hardware,"
      and "God-given" attitude;

of taking the sacrament,
      bread and water, served
up by young deacons, all boys.

      The message came through loud
and clear: Women are inferior.
      And God likes it that way.

Silly Me

I refused to believe it.
Not only that, but I began
to resent the whole idea.

I had watched women crushed
beneath the weight
of dreams, smashed.

I had seen them bow down
before their husbands,
and not just figuratively.

I had witnessed bone-chilling
abuse, no questions,
no help, no escape.

All in the hopes
that when they died,
and reached up from the grave,

their husbands would grab
hold, tug hard, and allow
them to enter heaven.

As I sat through that sacrament
meeting, observing those women
smile and nod and kowtow,

my warped little mind
wondered if any of them ever
dreamed about really hot guys.

Somehow, I Couldn't Reconcile

Any of the LDS viewpoint
with a "wake up, tingly all
over, and bathed in a cool
sheen of sweat" kind of dream.

I considered talking to Jackie
about it. We were really each
other's best friends.
What else could we be?

Thick as mud, Mom always
said, and why not?
We shared siblings,
cohabited a double bed,

confided concerns,
divvied responsibilities.
Traded secrets.
Plotted the future.

Besides, who else
but my closest sister
could understand
the uncertainty of our lives?

Still, I was pretty sure
she couldn't relate
to spicy dreams about
Justin Proud.

Mom was out. Jackie
was out. I tried to
think of a friend who
might understand.

Oh Yes

I had a few friends,
        upstanding Mormon girls all.
Becca and Emily
        lived just around the corner.
We'd known each other
        since primary, and
before too many sisters
        made it nearly impossible,
we used to play together.
        In grade school we walked
to the bus together, sat as if glued
        together, giggled together.
Confided hopes and dreams.

But our moms knew each
        other, our dads held
church callings together.
        Once things at the Von Stratten
house started to dive south,
        I didn't dare talk to Becca
or Emily about them.
        Once baby detail fell more
and more to me, I didn't
        have time for outside activities.

Becca played outstanding
        soccer. Emily sang outstanding
soprano. I was an outstanding
        diaper-changing machine.

So we'd chat a bit at church,
        walk to class together,
discuss a hunk du jour,
        without believing he might
ever belong to any of us.
        Sometimes we'd go to church
activities together, but in
        the final analysis, we had
very little in common.
        Not like Jackie and me,
who had almost everything
        in common and no secret
worth keeping from each
        other. At least not then.

But Neither Becca

Nor Emily could possibly
answer my questions about
maintaining all manner of decency
while a person dreams.

So I decided to pose the question in seminary.

Wait. Do you know about seminary?
See, come high school, Latter-Day
teenagers spend an hour each weekday
morning, before the first bell rings,

being reminded of Who We Are.

We met at Brother Prior's house.
Dad drove me on his way to work.
Afterward, I could walk to school
with other good Mormon kids,

the "right kind" to have as friends.

Brother Prior repeated scriptures,
though we'd heard them a thousand
times already. It was his job to reinforce
our values and keep our testimony strong.

He did not encourage hard questions.

Once, after one of Dad's really bad
Saturday nights left Mom too battered to chance
Sunday services, I arrived at Brother Prior's
on Monday morning, weighted heavily.

I didn't hear more than a select few words:

respect . . .
expect . . .
require . . .

Finally, I jumped up. "Excuse me,
Brother Prior, but is it okay for a man to . . ."
Nine of my peers turned and I caught
something strange in their eyes,

something . . .
knowing.

Did They Know

About Dad and his deepening
relationship with Johnnie
Walker Black scotch whiskey?

How, despite the church's
prohibition of all things alcoholic,
he only drank more and more?

Did they know why Mom rarely
left the house and often wore
dark glasses to services?

How she never said a word,
and neither did we, though
we knew we really should?

How, no matter what happened
the night before, the next day Mom
and Dad would be tandem in bed?

How Jackie and I would get up,
straighten up, dress the little ones
and take them outside to play?

Did they know how maybe once
a year Dad would confess to
the bishop, promise to do better?

> Or how every time he fell
> back off the wagon his rage
> only seemed to grow deeper?

I tried to find answers in their
eyes. But all I found behind
their blinks were blank walls.

> I couldn't cough out the rest
> of my question. Instead I decided
> to look like a total dolt.

". . . Never mind. I forgot
what I was going to say.
It wasn't important, anyway."

Later, However

My cowardice came back to haunt me,
wrapped in Mom's muffled screams.

And now, the dream thing preyed on my mind.
I'd never been so impressed by a dream.

I mean, it wasn't a nightmare, not at all.
But its honesty ran chills down my spine.

Was it really something I wanted, deep down?
Would I rot in the grave because I wanted it?

So I stood up and dared to ask Brother Prior,
"Are we responsible for our dreams?"

Serena's jaw dropped. Marla giggled.
Mike and Trevor poked each other.

> Brother Prior looked completely perplexed.
> *I'm sure I don't know what*
>
> *you mean, Pattyn. Let's get back
> to our scriptures, shall we?*

Maybe It Was the "Shall"

Maybe it was just his obnoxious tone,
but I decided not to let it drop.

"But *are* we? I mean, if we dream,
let's say, about killing someone,
will God hold us responsible?"

> Did *you dream about
> killing someone?*

"No . . ." I fixed my eyes on his.
". . . but I did dream about sex."

The girls gasped. The boys laughed.
Brother Prior turned the color
of Mom's rhubarb-cherry pie.

> *Uh. Um. Well, that's fairly
> normal for someone your age.*

"What do you mean, 'fairly'?
And how does God feel about it?"

I was center stage, everyone
waiting to see what came next.
But for once I didn't care.

*Uh. Um. Well, I can't really
speak for God, Pattyn.*

"Really?" Then what, exactly,
was I sitting there for?

Journal Entry, March 23

Brother Prior is an idiot. And I'm
supposed to swallow his garbage
like it doesn't even taste bad.
Well, it stinks! Ask him about
Joseph Smith, he can recite
an entire oral history.
Ask him about dreams,
he pretends like he
doesn't have them.
Ask him about God . . .

I'm not sure he even believes
God exists.

Do I?
Does Mom?

Does Dad? I mean, really?
I know his past haunts him.
But if he truly believes
he and God are brothers,
meant to live together
in the Great Beyond,
can't he ask for a hand,
a way to silence his ghosts,

without Johnnie WB?
Or is his drinking sin
enough to make his Heavenly
Sibling turn His back?

The Next Day in Chemistry Lab

Mr. Trotter partnered
me with Tiffany Grant.
Her style was low-ride
jeans, belly-baring tops
and designer tennis shoes.

> *Oh good,* she cooed. *I get
> the smart one. Guess I won't
> start any fires today.*

Tiffany and Bunsen
burners were incompatible.
One time she singed the ends
of her perfect hazelnut hair.
My life was in danger!

> Tiffany poured water
> into a beaker. *You light
> the burner, Pat.*

Pat? That's what you did
to a dog's head. Part of me
wanted to say something
nasty. The cautious part won
out. "Please call me Pattyn."

> *That's actually a pretty name.*
> Her carrot-colored fingernails
> tapped against the counter.

Actually? As I added salt
to the beaker, Mr. Trotter
stepped out of the room.
Not two minutes later, guess
who walked through the door?

Justin Sauntered Over

Totally

        defining the word
        "saunter." For
        one completely

insane

        minute, I forgot
        about my lab
        partner and actually

thought

        he was coming
        over to talk to me.
        A fine, prickly

mist

        of sweat broke
        out all over my body,
        chilled by a jolt of

reality.

        Justin barely glanced
        at me before turning
        to Tiffany.

            Hey, gorgeous.
            Still on for Saturday?

Zap!

I was
nobody. So
why would I think
he wanted to talk to me?
And why wouldn't he want
to talk to Tiffany, who had
everything I would never have:
beauty, money, confidence (okay, conceit)?

Justin
slid his arm
around her tiny
waist, walked his long
fingers along her exposed
skin. I couldn't keep from watching
out of the corner of one eye, jealousy
seeping from my pores, sourdough perfume.

Tiffany
pretended to be
offended. "Stop it,
Justin. Everybody's
watching. And what if Mr.
Trotter comes back right now?"
But she didn't try to move his hand
and in fact, curled tighter against his torso.

Zap!
I was nobody.
Someday, would
another nobody slide his
arm around my substantial waist,
walk his hand up under my homemade
blouse? And would I draw back into the curve
of him, close my eyes, and take pleasure in his heat?

Daydreams Bite

At least in chemistry lab.
As my body broke out
in a bone-chilling sweat,
Mr. Trotter snuck up behind me.

> *Don't add the oil yet, Pattyn.*
> *Pay attention!*

I jumped, knocking over
the beaker of salt water,
with an oil float.
Exxon Valdez in miniature!

> *I'm surprised, Pattyn.*
> *Usually you're so careful.*

Usually I wasn't confronted
by sex dreams in the flesh;
living, breathing sex dreams,
with a Tiffany twist.

> *Clean up your mess. Then*
> *perhaps you'd better start over.*

I turned to apologize to my lab
partner, but she and Justin
had slipped out the door, no doubt
before Mr. Trotter returned.

Timing is everything.

Timing Was Poor

The next afternoon—Friday
afternoon. Mom asked me
to run out back to the storage
shed to get a jar of spaghetti sauce
from our stash of emergency supplies.

Imagine, storing enough
food and water to nurture a family
of nine for a year, "when the shit
hit the fan and it all came crashing down."
Another Latter-Day Saints edict.

Dad's aged Subaru was already
parked out back. Some Fridays he
got off early from his job, working
security at the state legislature.
He saw it as a decent occupation,
which paid the bills
and provided insurance and retirement.

I saw it as kind of boring most
of the time, with the odd takedown
to provide a rush of adrenaline
and a blush of importance.

Anyway, somewhere between stacks
of batteries, boxes of bullets,
and countless cans
of tuna, Spam, and beans
was Dad's stash of Johnnie WB.

Weeknights, he'd duck outside
for an after-dinner belt. Just enough
to allow sleep. But come Friday
afternoon, he'd head straight for his
good buddy Johnnie. They partied hearty.

And the party had already started.

As I Approached the Shed

I heard his voice, thick
as caramel on his tongue.

> *Leave me alone. I*
> *can't help you now.*

Part of me wanted to run.
Part of me had to listen.

> *Goddammit, Molly,*
> *go away. Please.*

Molly. His first wife.
The true love of his life.

> *I miss Dwight too,*
> *you know I do.*

Dwight, who carried soldier
in his genes.

> *I couldn't tell him not*
> *to go, could I?*

Their first son, killed in a
firefight in Somalia.

> *What's that? Fuck Douglas,*
> *the friggin' fag.*

Their second son, until he
came out of the closet.

> *No, dammit. No son of mine*
> *will take it from another man.*

So he told him never to show
his face nearby again.

> *But you didn't have to do*
> *what you did!*

One son dead, the other
shunned, Molly folded.

> *Don't you know how*
> *much I miss you?*

Put a .357 into her mouth,
pulled the trigger.

> *Oh God, Molly,*
> *please stop crying.*

The Long Pause

Told
me it
wasn't
Molly who
was sobbing.
I'd never heard
my father cry
before.   How
                  many
                  times
               had I tried
            my best to hate
         that complicated
         man. But this
            tiny piece   of me
                              kept
                              thinking
                           back to another,
                        happier time, when
                     Mom loved Dad.
                  And me. And
                     Dad loved

Mom.
And
me. At
least as much
as he could with
that dead, cold space
growing inside him,
that place no   amount
of love
could
ever settle into.
That impenetrable
arctic land where his
ghosts had carried
his heart.

I Sort of Remember

Crawling up into Daddy's lap,
when Dad was still

                Daddy,

nodding my head against
his chest, soaking in
the comfort of his heat,

                listening

to the *thump . . . thump,*
somewhere beneath muscle
and breastbone. I remember
his arms, their sublime

                encircling,

and the shadow of his voice:
I love you, little girl.
Put away your bad dreams.

                Daddy's here.

I put them away. Until
Daddy became my nightmare,
the one that came

                home

from work every day
and, instead of picking me
up, chased me far, far away.

I Wasn't Sure Which Dad

I would find inside the shed,
although I had a pretty good
idea he wouldn't want me
to witness him crying—not
the macho man he wanted
the world to believe him to be.

Truth was, in his day, Dad
was about as bad as they came.
Way back in the late sixties, when
everyone else ducked the draft,
Dad ran right down and joined up.
Wanted to "waste gooks."

Left Molly, his wife of only
a few weeks, at home while
he toured Vietnam in an A-4
Skyhawk, a not-so-lean killing
machine designed to deliver
maximum firepower.

And Dad was just the man—
boy—to deliver it.

He came home long enough
to get Molly pregnant, then joined
up for a second tour of duty.
Dwight was almost two
before he met his dad.

Sad.

Not Dad's Fault

Any more than I'm entirely to blame
for what I've become. It's all in the molding.

Dad's dad, Grandpa Paul, with the scary
gray eyes (scary because, if you dared
look into them, somehow you'd see
the things he'd seen),

served his country too, "slappin' Japs"
in World War II.

He slapped them good, taking a patriot's
revenge for buddies lost at Pearl Harbor.
Justified. Glorified.

Deified with a Medal of Honor and a Purple
Heart for the leg lost to shrapnel.

Grandpa Paul refused prosthetics,
said living with a stump was no more
than the Good Lord's daily reminder
of wrongs still in need of righting.

Mistakes in need of correction.

But It Only Takes One Leg

(And what's located next to it)
to create a whole brood of kids.
Dad was number three of five.

Hard to stand out

when you're number three.
Hard to be the apple of your
mother's eye. Harder still

to gain the affection

of a father whose love for any
living thing was lost along
with his buddies and his leg.

Even Grandma Jane,

his wife till death did part them,
prematurely, would never regain
the love she lost to battle scars.

Distance begets distance begets . . .

Well, that was yet to be decided.

One Thing Already Decided

```
Was
    spaghetti
            for
                dinner.
                Mom
                  was
        waiting
        for
    the                     Now
  sauce,                     Dad
    Dad                        had
      had                          never
      already                  laid
      hit                      a
    the                        hand
  sauce,                       on
      and                      us          But
        it                     girls        I
      wasn't                  (not         didn't
          tomato.            so           want           had.
                             far,          to            Plus,
                               any-       disturb         I
                             way).        his            knew
                             I            demons          he
                               wasn't              any           was
                               afraid             more           sick
                                 of               than           of
                               that.              he             spaghetti.
                                                  already
```

I Started to Sing

Loud, so he'd know I was coming.
To make double-sure, I clomped
across the wooden walkway,
sounding pretty much like a cow.

> Dad was too far gone to care.
> He had quit talking to Molly.
> Now he whispered to the
> other spirits who crowded his life.

> *You're dead, you fucking gooks.*
> *North, South, who could tell? You*
> *all looked alike from the air. Go on*
> *back to hell. Your babies need you.*

I creaked the door open. "Dad?
It's me, Pattyn." Didn't want him
to think I was a gook in the flesh.
"Mom needs some spaghetti sauce."

> The shed fell silent for a second
> or two as Dad tried to collect
> himself. When he finally did,
> my words sank in.

Spaghetti? Again? You tell your
mother I won't be sharing
the dinner table tonight. I'm
going lookin' for Julia Child.

I didn't dare mention she
was dead, although he probably
would have felt right at home
in her company.

Even Without Dad

The dinner table remained
eerily quiet, as if each of us,
even the little ones,
intuited what was to come.

Mom rarely expected Dad
for dinner on Friday night.
Johnnie, it seemed,
was always on a diet.

Usually we chatted
and giggled, hoping
Dad would wander in late,
settle down on the sofa,

and watch mindless
TV until he and Johnnie
fell deep, deep asleep.
Relatively harmless.

Often, it happened
that way. We'd all tiptoe
off to bed, leaving
Dad to his nightmares.

In the morning, we'd wake
to irrefutable proof of Mom's
undying love—Dad, snoozing
on the couch, under a blanket.

But on That Night

Dad staggered in, eyes eerily lit.
                The corners of his mouth foaming spit.
                His demons planned an overnight stay.
Mom motioned to take the girls away,

hide them in their rooms, safe in their beds.
                We closed the doors, covered our heads,
                as if blankets could mute the sounds of his blows
or we could silence her screams beneath our pillows.

I hugged the littlest ones close to my chest,
                till the beat of my heart lulled them to rest.
                Only then did I let myself cry.
Only then did I let myself wonder why

Mom didn't fight back, didn't defend,
                didn't confess to family or friend.
                Had Dad's demons claimed her soul?
Or was this, as well, a woman's role?

When the House Fell Quiet

Jackie and I whispered
very late into the night.

We talked about Mom.

She used to be so pretty,
Jackie sighed.

"Too many worries will
take your pretty away."

We talked about Dad.

*Do you think he's an . . .
alcoholic?*

"Do you think he can stop?
Then he's an alcoholic."

We talked about the two of them.

*Why does he do it?
Why doesn't she leave him?*

"Where would she go
that he couldn't follow?"

Why doesn't she tell?

"Who would care?"

After a While, She Asked

Do you ever wish you were
someone else?

"All the time.
Who'd want to be me?"

I would. You're smarter
than most, Patty.

"What's so great about
being smart?"

God has something in mind
for you. Something special.

"You think God would let
a girl do something special?"

Not every girl. Maybe just
you. You're different.

I felt different. Still,
"How do you know?"

I can see it in your eyes
when they stop and stare.

"What?" What could she
see, buried inside of me?

You're not like the rest
of us. You're not afraid.

That Made Me Think

I felt angry,

frustrated.

I felt I didn't belong, not in my
church, not in my home, not

in my skin.

Amidst the chaos, I felt

alone,

in need of a friend instead of
a sister, someone detached from

my world.

The "woman's role" theory

disgusted me.

I would soon be a woman, and I
knew I could never perform as

expected.

I was tired of my mom's

submission

to her religion, to her husband's
sick quest for an heir,

to his abuse.

I was sick of my dad, of

reaching for

him as he fell farther away
from us and into the arms of

Johnnie WB.

Something bigger drew

        my worry:

the creeping cold in my own
famished heart, emptiness

        expanding.

Some days I was only

        sad,

others I straddled depression.
But I was definitely

        not afraid.

Which Brought Me Up Short

If I wasn't afraid, I must be crazy.
Right? Didn't dads who hit moms
usually wind up hitting their kids,
too? (And sometimes worse?)

Or maybe that's what I wanted?
Did some insane little piece of me
think even that might be better
than no relationship with my father at all?

And why wasn't I afraid of the path
already plotted for me—mission work,
early marriage, brainwashing
my own passel of Latter-Day kids?

Did that same mixed-up part of my brain
somehow believe I could circumvent
all I'd ever been groomed for?
Perhaps all I was really good for?

God has something special in mind for you.
I knew deep down she was right.
But how would I ever find out,
mired there in the Von Stratten bog?

I Tried Asking Him Once

"God, what do you have
in mind for me?"

        I listened really hard,
        opened my ears and heart.

I looked for signs,
in places expected—and not.

        Expected: church, seminary,
        the Book of Mormon.

Unexpected: clouds, constellations,
wind-sculpted patterns in sand.

        But I never heard His answer,
        never got one little hint of His plans.

Which was either good or bad,
depending on your point of view.

        Because if He would have mentioned
        then what He had in mind,

I would have thanked Him for His
faith in me, then tucked my tail and run.

I Slithered Out of Bed

The next morning, hungry
for a little target practice—
a great way to blow off steam.

        I walked a long way out
        into the desert, absorbing
        the faux spring day.

Every year, two or three weeks
of fine weather interrupted
our winter deep freeze,

        teasing soil into thaw
        and stream into melt
        and plants into breaking leaf.

It was all a game, all for show,
as if God understood we needed
to defrost our spirits, too.

        As I walked, I thought
        about Dad, at home, using
        this fabulous day to tune his car.

When I was little, he used
to hike this very route,
lugging his favorite rifle.

I always begged to go along,
mostly as a way to spend
some time alone with him.

I was ten before he finally
said yes, and didn't I feel
like the favored one?

Dad and I went out to the shed.
He unlocked the cabinet
that housed his guns.

Hunting rifles. Shotguns.
Pistols. And one little .22
"peashooter," just right for me.

This was Dwight's, Dad said.
I don't suppose he'd mind,
long as you take good care of it.

He Made Me Carry My Own Gun

I knew he would have made Dwight
do the same, so I tried my best
                    not to complain. But by the time

we'd walked far enough so an errant shot
had only sand or sage to hurt,
                    that little peashooter felt like a cannon.

Dad showed me how to load it, flip
the safety, sight in the tin-can target.
                    Squeeze the trigger, little girl. Don't pull.

I pulled, of course. The barrel lifted,
lofting the bullet high and wide right.
                    Try again. Take your time.

I brought the .22 to my shoulder,
willed my aching arms to quit shaking.
                    Level the sight. Breathe in. Ease the trigger.

The shot wasn't dead center, but it hit
the top of the can with a satisfying *BLING!*
                    Better. Do it again. Concentrate. And relax.

Concentrate. Level the sight. Breathe in.
Ease the trigger. And relax?

> *BLAP!* The can somersaulted across the sand.

Pride swelled till I thought I'd burst.
But my smile slipped at Dad's reality check.

> *Not bad. Pretty good, in fact. For a girl.*

After That

I still tagged along with Dad sometimes.
He taught me a lot on those outings:

how to account for the wind's contrary
nature, its irritating whims;

how to move silently across the sand,
a no-brainer compared to the jungle;

how to aim slightly in front of a moving
target, assuming a straight-on run.

I even brought home a rabbit or two
for Mom's always-hungry stew pot.

But I could never be Dwight.
And Dad never let me forget it.

Finally, I did my target shooting alone.

Killing Bunnies

Was not the point,
   drawing blood,
     watching life ebb,
       pulse by pulse.
         No, that wasn't
Neither was feeding   it at all.
  the family—not
   my job, for sure.
     Dad and Mom
      made us kids,
       only right
And the whole   they fed us.
  skinning and
   gutting thing,
    well, that
      was enough
       to make your
Truly, though,   skin crawl.
  the attraction
   was more than
     just being good—
      really good—
       at something
        for a change.

The lure of my
     little peashooter
         was in its gift
             to me, in the way
                 only it could
                     make me feel.

Powerful.

If You've Never Shot a Gun

You can't understand
how it feels in your hands.
Cool to the touch, all its venom
coiled inside, deadly,
like a steel-scaled serpent.

                    Awaiting your bidding.

You select its prey—paper,
tin, or flesh. You lie in wait,
learn that patience is the killer's
most trustworthy accomplice.
You choose the moment.

                    What. Where. When. Decided.

But the how is everything.
You lift your weapon,
ease it into place, cock it
to load it, knowing the
satisfying *snitch* means

                    a bullet is yours to command.

Now, make or break,
it's all up to you. You
aim, knowing a hair either
way means bull's-eye or miss.
Success or failure.

                    Life or death.

You have to relax,
convince your muscles
not to tense, not to betray
you. Sight again. Adjust.
Don't become distracted by

the heat of the hunt.

Instinct takes over.
You shoot and adrenaline
screams as your target shreds
or the rabbit drops. And for
one indescribable instant,

you are God.

By the Time

I started high school,
I was a dead-on shot.

I spent a lot of Saturdays
maintaining that distinction.

You might think
a teenager's parents

would take notice
when she disappeared

into the desert
for hours at a time

(with a rifle and purloined
ammo, no less!).

But Mom only
noticed diapers

in need of changing.
By then, I could bribe

Jackie to do it.
All it took was my

own silence about her less
than "saintly" behaviors.

And as for Dad,
well, he and Johnnie

had started to buddy up
almost all day, almost

every Saturday.
How he sobered up

by Sunday morning
was a complete mystery.

On That Saturday

He'd already started, which
made me thankful for my solo
time in the silent desert.

I trudged along, brain only
partially engaged, and about halfway
to my favorite place,

my mind veered from Dad
back to chemistry lab. Jealousy
rushed, hot, through my veins.

But why? I mean, it wasn't
like Justin had ever *really* been
mine. Dreams were only dreams.

It wasn't like my life had
changed at all, and maybe
that was part of the problem.

Because something inside
me was different. Shifting,
like a tide or sand dune.

That something was growing,
stretching, taking shape
beneath my skin.

And I wondered if very
soon it might blow
me apart at the seams.

I Thought About That

As I set up a long, thin row of V8 cans
(single serving, not the big, easy-to-hit kind).

Loaded my peashooter, took aim, and . . .
missed wide with the first shot, high with the second.

Checked my sights; they didn't look bent. Tried again.
Skittered up dirt, nicked a can with the ricochet.

Timing, I heard my dad's voice in my head.
Then he added, *What could you expect from a girl?*

That did the trick. I settled down into my zone, took
out that row of cans one by one, not a single miss.

As I lined them up again, an annoying mechanical
whine broke the morning's tranquility.

Louder. Louder. A three-pack of quadrunners
sprinted closer and closer across the sage-studded sand.

I didn't dare take another shot until they passed
by and rode off to disturb distant eardrums.

Instead they slowed, drew even, and stopped.
Three guesses who drove the first quad.

One guess who rode behind him.

Justin Took Off His Helmet

        Climbed off his quad.
        Tiffany did likewise.

The others—Brent and Melina
on quad #2, Derek solo on #3—
remained astraddle.

        Hey, Pat, tittered Tiffany,
        Watcha doing all the way out here?

I stood, .22 by my side,
taking deviant satisfaction
as her eyes went wide.

        Justin surveyed the rifle.
        Target shootin', huh?

My voice tried to stick behind
my tonsils, but somehow I
choked out a solid, "Uh-huh."

        He slithered over.
        You any good with that thing?

I nodded, heart hiccuping
at his proximity. "Good
enough, I guess."

He moved behind me, stood way
too close. *Okay, then. Show me.*

I couldn't, not with my
hands trembling like saplings
in a summer zephyr.

Justin noticed, whispered in my ear.
I'm not making you nervous, am I?

He Was Making Tiffany Nervous

Or maybe I was.
      She shifted from
foot to foot. *C'mon, Justin.*
                Wait. I want to see her shoot.

Okay, I'd show him.
      I took two steps forward,
sighted in, steadied . . .
                Damn! Six clean shots. Not bad. . . .

Here it came. The old
      "for a girl" addendum.
But no, he said instead,
                Can I have a try?

It was the most attention
      he'd ever paid to me.
I could take more. "Why not?"
                Hey, Tiff. Set up the cans.

She was irritated, and it
      showed, but she did
as instructed. Justin took aim . . .
                Shitfire! One out of six.

As the others climbed off
              their quads, I suggested ways
to improve his performance.
                    Three out of five. Right on!

Now everyone wanted
              a turn. Everyone, that
is, except for Tiffany.
                    Come on, Tiff. Give it a try.

You know I hate guns.
              They're stupid. She stood
off to one side, simmering.
                    Fuck you, bitch. This is fun.

We Had Fun

For an hour, maybe
more. For once, I

lost

track of time,

found

I didn't care what

time

it was, not in this amazing

space

I was somehow in.
After a while, I didn't

even

feel like the

odd

girl

out

of this decidedly

in

clique. In fact, I felt more "in"
than Tiffany, who stood

off

by herself, carrying

on

about firearm

danger

and her personal

safety.

I didn't feel

bad

about being with boys,
and thinking not quite

good

thoughts about them.
My heart insisted it wasn't

wrong

that they weren't Mormon, either,
though my head said it wasn't exactly

right.

I Barely Flinched

When Brent pulled out a pack
of cigarettes, lit one for Melina,
another for himself.
"Hey," squealed Tiffany,
"what about me?"

>Justin handed me the rifle
>and fished inside his pocket
>for his own nicotine stash.
>He gave one to Tiffany,
>offered one to me.

Cigarettes are high on
the list of Latter-Day sins.
The smoke, hanging like
smog, made me queasy. So
why was I tempted to join in?

>Watching them inhale
>poisonous fumes, I shook
>my head. But maybe I looked
>envious, because Derek pulled
>closer. *Have you ever tried?*

Don't be stupid! said
Tiffany. *Don't you know?*
She's a Mormon.
The word seethed from
her mouth like spittle.

> Derek measured me with
> cool blue eyes.
> *Could have fooled me.*
> *I didn't know Mormon*
> *girls were so pretty.*

Okay, it was a line, but
it put me in a heady new space.
No one had ever called
me pretty before.
Not even my mom and dad.

Derek Wasn't Exactly Justin

Not pinup gorgeous
or hot bod built,
but he wasn't bad:

> Tall,
> around
> 6'2,
> slender,
> with
> black
> coffee
> hair
> and
> vivid
> blue
> eyes
> that
> could
> pierce
> you
> through.

His hands were soft.
I discovered that when
he brushed my cheek.

*So what's a nice Mormon
girl like you doing in a place
like this?*

We Laughed at the Old Joke

And talked and talked
about nothing much,
while the others kept
their lips busy in much
more interesting ways.

Lightweight conversation
with a guy of Derek's
caliber, clique-wise,
was way beyond my
loveliest fantasy.

What was I doing here?
With them? With him?

And why his sudden interest
in me? I mean, we weren't
exactly strangers, but
we'd never exactly
been friends, either.

Looking back, I guess
it was kind of strange.
At least for me, who'd
never been that close
to a boy before.

But I liked him.
I liked his optimism,
his easy way with words.
Most of all, I liked
how he made me feel

that I—Pattyn
Von Stratten—

mattered.

After a While

Brent pulled Melina to her feet,
dragged her off for a private minute or ten.

Justin winked at Tiffany. *Sounds like
the right idea to me.*

I had a general idea of what they had
in mind. Envy jolted.

> *You like him, huh?*

I gulped down the truth and said
simply, "He's not mine to like."

> *That doesn't stop most people.*

"I'm not most people, Derek."
Even if I did, in fact, like him.

> *So I've noticed.*

With a drift of tobacco and sun-scented
skin, he moved very close to me.

> *What I can't figure out . . .*

My heart tap-danced as he slipped
his arm around my shoulder.

> *is why I never really
> noticed you before.*

With His Arm Around Me

I asked what happened to Carmen,
the girl he'd been linked
with practically forever.

> He shrugged. *Don't know.*
> *Guess we grew apart.*
> Then he asked, *What about you?*

I knew what he meant, but not
how to respond. So I said,
"What about me . . . what?"

> He smiled and his hand
> toyed with my hair. *Any good*
> *Mormon guys on your line?*

On my line? I had to laugh.
"No way," I admitted. "I don't
think I've got the right bait."

> Derek turned my face so I
> couldn't avoid his eyes.
> *Don't sell yourself short, Pattyn.*

Oh God! This was crazy.
I thought he just might try
to kiss me, when Tiffany yelled,

*Shit! It's almost four. My
mom is going to kill me.
Let's go, you guys!*

Almost Four!

I'd never   stayed
out in the   desert
this long,   and I
had a good   half-
hour walk   home.
What would   my own
mom say?   Anything?
I didn't want   to think
about Dad at all, although he and Johnnie were
          no doubt
          pretty
          cozy by
          then.
          Luckily
          (happily),
          Derek
          offered
          to save
          me some
          time: *Can*
          I give you
          a ride?

No Spare Helmet

Derek promised to go slow
and told me to hang on tight.

Rifle in my right hand,
I wrapped my left around

his waist, leaned my face
against his back.

If I turned my head,
I could hear his heartbeat,

a steady drum, unlike my
own hummingbird pulse.

It was all too incredible,
like a scene from a movie

or a page from a book, one
you read again and again.

My head swam with the scent
of him, the promise of him,

and I never once stopped
to think that being with him

could mean the end of Pattyn
as I knew her up until that day.

He Dropped Me Off

Right where the dirt trail
segued into pavement.

I'll see you Monday, okay?

Was that a promise?
A generic blow-off?

I watched him motor
off, then started for home.

Slowly. Thinking. Trying
to process the weight of my day.

For once, I didn't feel
like an outcast, a major loser.

Whether or not Derek
ever spoke to me again,

I had fit in with the in
crowd, if only for a while.

Not only that, but one of the in
crowd had put his arm around me.

Maybe almost kissed me.
And I would have let him.

So what did that make me?

When I Got Home

        None of that mattered.
Reality
            rushed in
            around me.
Crushed
            me, like the watery
            weight of the deepest sea.
            Jackie ran out to warn
            me Dad had already
drowned
            himself in Johnnie WB,
            Mom had asked where
            to find me, and the kids were
            yelling for me. I went inside,
            all remnants of the newfound me
smothered.

Later On

I lay listening to the music
        of sleep. Inhale. Exhale.
A symphony of breathing,
        hearty, steady, frail.

I shimmied out of bed,
        tiptoed to the bathroom.
Listening for movement,
        I sat a moment in the gloom.

Then I turned on the light
        above the narrow mirror,
needing to analyze
        the face that appeared.

Funny, but I rarely
        studied my reflection,
rarely allowed myself
        such tedious inspection.

But somconc—a boy—
        had likcd my face
and I liked that he liked it.
        Had I tumbled from grace?

What had he seen that
        I'd always missed before?
Plain amber eyes. Straight auburn hair.
        Was there something more?

Something indefinable,
        that somehow made me pretty,
like how brilliant neon lights
        cheer the dirty streets of a city?

All I saw in the mirror's depths
        was a spatter of freckles, sharp angles,
too much flesh here, not enough
        there, imperfect teeth, dry skin, and tangles.

So what had he seen in me?

I Pondered That

All the next day—through breakfast
and the pre-services scramble;

through three hours of Mutual
and droning testimony.

My thoughts were far from pure.

Through après-services chatter,
squashing into the car for the short ride home.

I couldn't turn off my brain.
What did yesterday mean?

Anything?

Or was it all just another dream,
one I'd dreamed while awake?

Three days ago, the only boy
on my mind was Justin.

He was a dream too. A safe dream.

—

Safe, because he was unattainable,
something to adore from afar.

Like a snow-drenched mountain
or an evening star.

But what about Derek?

*J*ournal Entry, March 26

Derek Colthorpe
told me
I'm pretty.
At least
I think
that's what
he told
me.
Pretty?
Me?

And he
told me
he'd see
me on
Monday.

Do
I
dare
believe
him?

I Didn't Dare

Hurt seemed too likely,
so on Monday I didn't
go looking for him.

I was a campus loner,
anyway, walking solo
between classrooms,
eating lunch with my sister.

Imagine my surprise
when he found me
at the noon break.

He smiled at Jackie.
Hi. Then he turned to me.
*Can I talk to you
for a minute?*

You should have seen
Jackie's face as the two
of us started away.

Derek steered me toward
a quiet spot. *Pattyn,
I know I'm not exactly
your type . . .*

He wasn't *my* type?
Where could this
be going but bad?

What I mean is, I'm
not a Mormon.
Maybe we're nothing
alike at all . . .

Understatement!
He was Chateaubriand.
I was hamburger.

He reached out
and touched my cheek.
But I'd really like
to see you again.

Not Sure

Whether it was his words
or his touch, but my face scorched.

So of course I came up with a really
great line. "Why?"

> Derek's smile narrowed.
> *Does that mean no?*

I shook my head. "No.
I just need to know why."

> *I don't know . . . because you're
> smart and funny and . . .*

Funny as in witty?
Or as in entertaining?

> *. . . and you're not trying
> to impress anyone.*

Mostly because I didn't
know I *could* impress anyone.

> *I happen to like you, Pattyn
> Isn't that a good enough reason?*

It was the perfect reason.
"I like you, too, Derek."

> *Okay, then. Friday night?
> Brent's having a party.*

A party? How could I
possibly swing that?

Derek misunderstood my dazed look. *Second thoughts already?*

"No, it's not that . . . not that at all. . . ."

You sure? 'Cause maybe this will change your mind. . . .

He Kissed Me

Not

demanding

passion.

just a

soft

caress.

an over-the-top,
hard

kiss, not even
a kiss hinting

No tongue, no spit,

sweet first
kiss, Derek's

full lips
gifting mine with a gentle

I thought I'd die on the spot.
(Later I wished I had.)

He Held My Hand

As he walked me back to where
Jackie still sat, doe-eyed.

Amazed.

He didn't know, but Jackie
did, that I was someone new.

Reborn.

The bell rang and he promised
to find me later.

Stunned,

I watched him go as Jackie
demanded, *What happened?*

Numb,

I wanted to tell her everything,
and I wanted to keep it all to myself,

frozen

inside, a perfect point of light
to focus on when everything fell dark.

As, of course, it must.

But I Told Her

A. She wouldn't let me keep it secret
and

B. I couldn't keep something as incredible
as that all to myself.

Jackie was almost as excited as I was.
He kissed you? Oh, Patty! He's so cute!

She even helped me hatch a plan to get out
of the house on Friday.

*There's a Ward dance on Friday. He can
pick you up there.*

I hardly ever went to Ward dances. Transportation
was always an issue.

*Mom can drop you off. We'll tell her you
have a ride home.*

Who knew my sister could be so devious?
And who knew if her plan would work?

It Worked Great

You see, coed church functions
were meant to relieve the teen
hormonal thing, with close
enough supervision
to assure the chastity thing.

> *I'm glad you want to go,*
> Mom said. *It's about time*
> *you discovered boys.*

If only she knew! Should she
know? Part of me felt guilty
that I hadn't confided. The smarter
part told me to keep my mouth
clamped tight. "What about Dad?"

> *Don't you worry about*
> *your father. Even he knows*
> *you have to grow up sometime.*

Growing up was one thing.
Discovering boys yet another.
But lying about the basic "who, when,
and where" was fundamentally wrong.
Did I have another choice?

> *A nice young man is in God's*
> *plans for you. Your father and I*
> *can't argue with that.*

Now *Mom* spoke for God. Did
He define "nice young man"
as an LDS boy with a testimony?
And would my parents argue
when I told them I wanted more?

> *And you're never going to find*
> *that young man sitting around*
> *the house every Friday night.*

Valid point, one *I* wouldn't argue
with, though I might have before.
I had my way out, my pass
to Brent's party. What would
happen after that, I had no clue.

*J*ournal Entry, April 1

Went to a party at Brent's
last night. Okay, more like a
drink-smoke-and-make-out fest.
But, hey, I was with Derek,
and for the first time in my life,
people looked at me with respect.
Maybe even envy.

The Ward dance started at seven.
Derek picked me up at eight.
By nine, he had convinced me
to try a sip of his beer. "Jesus
turned water into wine, didn't He?"
True, but Jesus had little to do
with LDS doctrine.

Still, I'd considered the possibility
all week. I'm probably already damned,
for dating a nonbeliever. What could a sip—
or three or four—of beer hurt?
Odd taste, not great, but drink
enough, who cares?

Loose. I let loose. Not all the way
loose, but I laughed at not-real-funny

jokes and let Derek pull me up into
his lap. And when he kissed me,
I full-on kissed back.
I even let his hands wander.

At first I said no, of course.
I really thought I wasn't at all
that kind of girl.
Guess what.
I am!

He was good, too. First he rubbed
my back. Then he lifted my hair
and kissed my neck, and I've never
had goose bumps like that before.

Then he slid his hands around
the front of me, lifting my breasts
and touching my nipples.
I wouldn't let him go under my blouse,
but even over my clothes,
the way he made my body
feel is hard to describe.
Alive.

On edge.
In need.
In danger of spontaneous combustion.
Virtue was the last thing on my mind.

Then his watch beeped. Eleven.
Early to leave, but I wasn't allowed
at that ball, anyway.
Derek took me home, and as we
kissed a very long good-bye,

I hoped everyone was asleep
so I'd be immune to questions.
Everyone was, except Jackie.
She wanted every last detail.
But how could I tell her all
she wanted to know without

admitting a crisis in faith?

I'd Done It

Lied

    my way out of the house.

Cheated

    certain punishment.

Stolen

    moments with Derek

invaded

    every waking thought,

infiltrated

    every dream.

    April passed like water

               lost

    in a downriver flow.

               Struggling

    to remain pure,

               surrendering

    ground to instinct,

               upsetting

    the scheme of things,

               forgetting

    more and more

    my feminine role.

I'd Like to Tell You

I'd fallen head   over heels in love
    with Derek. I did   feel something, but
        it wasn't the   hearts and flowers
            kind of love in my
                dog-eared
                books.

Looking back, it   seems I should
    have been in love   with him. We did
        all the things   two people in
            love were supposed
                to do. Maybe
                more.

I wanted to be   with him all the
    time, wanted the   taste of his lips
        on mine, his   roaming fingers
            on my hungry skin. His
                fire to thaw
                my ice.

But, though I was   very much in lust
    with him, I knew   from the start we
        were nothing   like "forever."
                    Maybe because forever
                        is such a scary
                            place.

Love or Lust

The need to be with Derek was intense.
Before school. During school.
After school. Instead of school. Saturdays.
Friday evenings, when I could.

I suppose I got careless about
who knew. And how much they knew.

Brent and Melina tolerated the tryst;
sometimes we rode quads together.
Justin and Tiffany mostly ignored us,
unless it was Derek's turn to score beer.

Becca and Emily pretended interest.
Later, I found out why.

Ms. Rose winked and slipped me her
personal copy of *Sappho's Leap*.
Hand in hand with her new boyfriend,
Carmen flashed smiles. Evil smiles.

I kept thinking once everyone got
used to the idea, things would come easier.

But Everything Came Harder

Seminary.
Sacrament meetings.
Sunday rituals.

Too many questions,
not enough answers.
Where did free will fit here?

Homerooms.
Classrooms.
Crowded hallways.

No place to hide to feed
the growing hunger.
Derek's. And mine.

Kitchen duty.
Diaper duty.
Daughterly duty.

Too many "had to"s,
left not enough time
for "want to"s.

Honesty.
Sobriety.
My virginity.

No way to regain
the first two, I almost
gave away the last.

One Problem with Alcohol

Is the more you drink it

the more you want it.

If a little lets you forget

a bit of your pain,

more lets you crawl into

a fuzzy space where

nothing hurts at all. Amen.

days—don't think the irony

Saturdays became drinking

Derek would meet me in

is one iota lost on me.

hand. First beer, then hard

the desert, painkiller in

on was no Johnnie WB.

stuff. The only thing I insisted

but something inside of me

Okay, it's a weird psychology

could hook me for good.

maintained only Johnnie

The higher I got, the harder

it got to hang on to my jeans.

Derek was skillful, coloring

his need to look like desire,

like I was all he'd ever wanted.

But every time I came really

close to just giving in, I

saw faces: Our bishop, reciting,

Better to die defending your

virtue than to live having lost

it without a struggle.

Brother Prior, *A true Mormon*

would rather bury a child

than see her lose her chastity.

My dad, *I'll kill the first*

SOB who lays a hand on you.

He Almost Got His Chance

The first Saturday in May.
I'd gone for my usual "target practice,"
    which by then, of course, meant an
    overheated session with Derek.

By noon, we had downed a half pint
of tequila, my buttons were askew,
    and Derek was trying to escape
    his zipper when I noticed
                a lone figure
                striding our way.
The purposeful gait was familiar.
"Derek, I think that's my dad."
    We struggled to straighten
    our clothes. Stashed the bottle.

Derek fished in his pocket for
breath mints as I picked up
    the rifle, took aim at nothing
    and let go a round.
                Shootin' sand,
                little girl?
My head spun from mescal and
jumping up too quickly.

I felt my face drain from red
to white. Derek's stayed red.

Aren't you going
to introduce us?

"Sorry! Dad, this is my friend
Derek. He was, uh, riding his quad
and he heard me shooting. I've
been giving him tips."

Riding your quad
and what else, boy?

Nothing, sir. Not a thing.
It's good to meet you, Mr. Von
Stratten. Patty has told
me a lot about you.

Did she tell you I named
her Pattyn?

Embarrassment branded my
cheeks. "Please be civil, Dad."
Dad looked at me like
I'd flat gone crazy.

Civil? You're out here
alone, doing God knows what . . .

Could he smell the tequila?
Were my buttons crooked?
          "We were just shooting
          targets . . ." I tried.

                    *I've heard all about
                    the two of you. . . .*

I swear, as I watched, Dad's
eyes grew black. Black.
          No more denial. "Okay,
          we've been dating."

                    *Interesting word for
                    what you've been doing.
                    You're finished here. Let's go.*

Dad pulled me away. I glanced
back over my shoulder.
          Derek shrugged, then
          started his quad.

                    *Damn good thing I
                    didn't catch you in the act.
                    You'd both be dead.*

My Friends Were Spies

Okay, maybe not exactly spies,
but Becca told her mom
about Derek and me.

Her mom, a notorious gossip,
spread the word at her
bridge club.

Sister Hobart soaked up
the news and came
blabbing to my mom.

My mom, who knew I'd
been seeing someone, was
shocked he wasn't Mormon.

Mom asked Bishop Crandall
for advice. He said to tell Dad,
then bring me in for counseling.

And that's why the next day at
sacrament meeting everyone made it
a point to stare when I walked through the door.

I Thought Dad's Rant Was Bad

I mean, he went on and on about
"what boys want" and what should happen
to boys if they manage to get what they want.
(A very ugly—not to mention painful—picture.)

Then he took away my rifle and told me
it would be a warm day in Antarctica
before I left the house again.

But Bishop Crandall, sitting smug
behind his tall teak desk, made me want
to scream. After an hour of his reminding
me of a woman's role,

I couldn't stand it anymore.
So I interrupted, "Is it a woman's role
to keep silent when her husband hits her?"

If I was looking for shock value,
I was looking in the wrong place.

> *Violence is never right. But a man
> has a duty to keep his wife in check.*

In check? Like Mom had ever asked
to go anywhere or do anything other
than wait on Dad and us kids?

He nailed me. *I hope you're not
accusing your father of such things.*

His tone made me waver. But I
didn't quite buckle. "What if I am?"

He leveled me. *Then I'd call you
a liar, with nothing to gain
and everything to lose.*

Censored

I went home,

withdrew

to my room,

sulked

all afternoon,

stressed

over what life
would be like

emptied

of Derek,

drained

of laughter,

strangled

by rules I'd
happily broken.

Depressed,

I put my pillow

over my head

forgetting
tears were

out of bounds

and let
myself cry.

Journal Entry, May 7

Life isn't fair.
I finally find
someone special
and they want
to take him
away from me.

Mom says I
should have
a boyfriend.
Why does he
have to be
Mormon?

Dad says I
shouldn't
even think
about boys.
Yeah, right.
What am I,
brain-dead?

Bishop Crandall
says one day
I'll have to obey

my husband.
No talk of love.
Can "love
and obey"
possibly go
together?

All I know
is, I'm old
enough to
make my own
decisions.
They won't
take Derek
away from me.
I won't
let them.

Turned Out

Derek gave me no other choice.
I saw him at school the next day,
smiled and waved him over.

> He half-waved back, turned,
> and walked off with Justin.

I ran to catch up with them.
"Derek? Can I talk to you?
What's the matter?"

> He spun. *The matter is you
> and your crazy father.*

"I don't think he acted so crazy."
Even if he did, what did that
have to do with me?

> *Give us a minute, okay, Justin?*
> Derek led me to a deserted corner.

I'd never had a boyfriend before,
so I'd never been dumped before.
But I knew where this was headed.

> *Patty, you know I care about you.
> But your dad made it very clear
> that I'd better leave you alone.*

I shook my head. "I never
heard anything like that, Derek."
Tears dammed up behind my lashes.

He came over to my house, Patty.
He said if I ever "bother" you again,
he'll kill me. And I believe him.

The tears leaked out. Derek
tried to hug me, but I pushed him
away. "So that's it? Just good-bye?"

Has to be. Anyway, it was bound
to happen sooner or later.
Sorry, Patty. See ya around.

Dismissed

I'm quiet-tempered by nature,
        but anger boiled up inside me.
                I didn't know who to be
                        angrier with—Dad,
                                or Derek.
What did he mean,
        "bound to happen"?
                Was it something he'd
                        planned all along?
                                      Who else knew?
I'd never used a cuss word
        before, but two or three
                popped into my mind
                        and I chose the worst.
                        "Fuck you!"

Derek just shook his head
        and kept on walking,
                and that only made
                      me angrier yet.
                        "I said, FUCK YOU!"

Everyone anywhere within
      shouting distance turned
            to stare at Pattyn
                 Von Stratten,
                        gone completely nuts.
Derek turned the corner,
      slithered right out of my
            life. And it was all
                 my dad's fault.
                        Wasn't it?

I Wasn't in Love with Derek

So why, all of a sudden, did I
feel like I couldn't live without him?

Why did I feel like I'd just taken
a cannonball to the gut?

Why did a sudden urge to hurt something
become so overwhelming?

I picked up my backpack, weighty
with books, did a 180 and let it fly.

In my wildest imagination, I could never
have guessed the trajectory it would choose.

Thunk! Tinkle . . . tinkle. My backpack went
straight through the library's picture window.

Good thing no one was on the other side.
Ms. Rose came running.

She saw me, tears reflecting my disbelief.
Her own eyes held pure shock.

"I'm so sorry, Ms. Rose . . ." I blubbered.
"I didn't mean . . . I mean . . . it just slipped . . ."

She told me she was sorry too, then
escorted me to the office.

I'd Never Been to the Office

Except to turn in absence notes
or take a phone call from home.
But never like this.

Never in shame.

And when Mr. Scoffield called
my mom, she couldn't believe
what he told her.

What she was hearing.

And when she passed on the news
to my dad—that he would be buying
a $500 window—he flipped.

Lost it completely.

For the first time ever,
he slapped me, hard,
like he'd done to Mom

a thousand times.

Defiance rose up like vomit.
I swung back and yelled,
"Don't ever do that again!"

He caught my arm.

Held it midair, and I found
in his eyes conflicting emotions—
something almost like apology,

and something very much like satisfaction.

Communication

Was never big in my house.
We sat down together over
dinner, but the only sound
you'd hear was crunching
and chewing and the little
ones asking for more, please.

We lived, all boxed up in
invisible containers. We
hardly knew the people
we called sister or father.
Jackie and I were the
exceptions to that rule.

But now even she and I
were afraid to reach out
to each other. I couldn't
blame her. Associate
with a pariah, you become
an outcast too. Don't you?

Dad always lived angry.
Now he lived furious.
Mom settled for passive;
she withdrew further into

her shell. The girls sensed
the need for quiet play.

As for me, I barely
said one word. Not
at home. Not at
school. For sure
not at seminary.

My little box
grew smaller
and smaller,
until there was

only part of
me inside.
The sad part.

A Week Went By

The school year was drawing
        to a close. Usually, I couldn't wait
for summer vacation. But what
        did I have to look forward to this year?

Jackie would be off to girls' camp, not
        a pleasant experience for me, but she
was jazzed, which only made me more
        jealous that I'd be locked up at home.

Not even the desert to take refuge
        in, unless I could somehow convince
Dad to loosen the reins. No stallions
        near this mare's pasture. Not anymore.

Every time I saw Derek at school,
        laughing with Justin or Brent,
while refusing to even acknowledge
        me, I got mad. Royally pissed.

Then came the day I saw him
        with Carmen, arm possessively
around her waist. As I watched,
        she reached up and kissed him.

A flare went off inside my head.
      I swear, my eyes filmed over, red.
Bishop Crandall told me Satan was
      to blame for the things I did with Derek.

Satan had nothing to do with that,
      of course, but he may have had something
to do with the utterly evil feelings
      that rose up inside me. Seeking escape.

I Followed Carmen and Derek

From a safe distance,
of course. I waited until
they split up. Derek went
into a classroom. Carmen
started toward the gym.

I caught up to her, fell in
beside her. "I thought you
and Derek were history."

> She stopped short.
> *No, you and Derek
> are history.*

This is where I think
the devil stepped in.
"Leave him alone, Carmen."

> She laughed.
> *No way, freak.
> Derek loves me.*

Then I laughed. Or Satan
did. "Derek only loves
Derek. He never loved you."

> *I suppose you think
> he loved you? He only
> used you for sex.*

Did he tell her that? Did
he tell everyone that?
"We never had sex."

> *That's not what he said.*
> *Not only that, he said*
> *it was lousy sex.*

I should have done what I
did to Derek, not Carmen.
But he wasn't standing there.

What I Did Was . . .

I cocked back
my fist, took
dead aim, and
punched her
straight in
the nose.

Her eyes went
wild. *Fuckin'
bitch! I'll
kill you.*

She and Dad
could team up.
I grabbed a
fistful of coal-
colored hair. "Oooh.
I'm so scared."

Carmen raked
my cheek with
deadly fingernails
and might have done
me worse than a six-
inch welt, except
right about then
her nose gushed.

I should have
run for first aid,
or at least felt
bad. Instead, I
said, "Your nose
is bleeding. Hey,
think it's broken?"

It Was Just a Hairline Fracture

But it was enough
        to get me suspended
    for the rest of the year.
                    And it was also enough
        to net a $1500 ER visit
                        for sweet little Carmen,
        which, as you may have guessed,
                    my dad had to pay for.
                        Well, actually, his homeowners'
        insurance had to pay it.

But, as he told me explicitly,
                My premiums will go up now,
        so it's still money out of my pocket.
                        Two thousand dollars in one week.
    What has happened to you, Pattyn?
                    Boys and booze. (So he had smelled
                        the tequila that day!)
        Broken windows, broken noses.

What kind of trouble have you become?

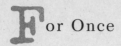# For Once

Mom blew it worse than Dad.
        In fact, she lost it completely.

                I work and slave, to make your life
            perfect. How could you do this to me?

Slave? Perfect? I might have argued.
        Instead I said, "I didn't do anything to you."

                Her face blossomed, rose red. *You*
            have stigmatized this entire family!

"Stigmatized? That's the biggest word
        I've ever heard you attempt, Mother."

                Her eyes flooded. *I'm not stupid. I*
            graduated high school, considered college.

"Then along came Dad. True love won
        you over. Please, don't make me gag."

                Pattyn! How can you be so nasty?
            Of course true love won me over.

"Sorry, Mom, but if there's one thing
        I've learned, watching you and Dad . . ."

Yes? What have you learned?

"Love is just another word for sex."

She Screamed

(This is the part
where she lost it.)

> *Sex? Sex! Tell*
> *me what you know about sex!*
> *Did that awful*
> *boy touch you? Put it in you?*

I couldn't resist
that lead-in.
"Put what in me?"

> *You know very*
> *well what I'm talking about.*
> *Did he take*
> *his pants off? Did you let him?*

Now it was a game.
"Let him? What if
I encouraged him?"

> *Pattyn Scarlet Von*
> *Stratten. Exactly what are you saying?*
> *Surely you can't*
> *mean you wanted to have sex?*

A vicious game.
"Don't you want
to have sex, Mom?"

> *Her face ignited*
> *flames. Wha . . . wha . . .*

"Or is it all about
overpopulating
this pitiful planet?"
                   She sputtered.
                   She fumed. She fizzled out.
"'Cause if that's
all it's about, you
can count me out."

If I'd Have Known Then

What I learned a few days later,
I might have made her squirm

        a little less.

Then again, maybe not.
My head felt constricted,
squashed in a vise of frustration,

        ready to pop like a blister.

All the questions I'd always
wanted to ask jumbled around in

        my brain, twisted into barbs.

"Don't worry, Mom. I know sex
leads to babies. You and Dad have
taught me that valuable lesson."

        I could have stopped there.

Might have stopped, had I noticed
how her face had turned ashen.

        Instead, I steamrolled her.

"You're like a blue-ribbon heifer,
Mom. Champion breeding stock,
always in heat for her bull."

        And almost regretted it

when she ran over to the kitchen
sink and heaved her lunch.

And truly regretted it
when she turned, shaky and pale,
flecks of vomit in her hair, and said,
I need to lie down for a while.

Later, Bishop Crandall Dropped By

The house to give me a stern
reprimand. He sat across
the cluttered table,

> playing with a paper clip.
> *Your parents are worried
> about you, Pattyn.*

I was worried about myself.
But I wasn't about to let him
know it. "Really?"

> *Really. What have you got
> to say for yourself? You've always
> been such a good girl.*

Good girl. Sit. Stay. Fetch.
Bristles rose up along my
spine. "Define good."

> *I don't appreciate your attitude,
> Pattyn. Fast and pray. Search your
> soul for the inequities in your life.*

"Any inequity in my life
began when I was born
female. Can you fix that?"

> *You'll have to fix that yourself,
> by concentrating on the things
> God expects of you.*

His two-faced rhetoric
was pissing me off. "You
mean like kissing your ass?"

He slammed his hand on the table.
I will not listen to that sort
of language. Apologize!

Behind me, I heard Mom
gasp. But I was on a roll.
"I'm sorry, Bishop.

I'm sorry I ever believed
you might have something
worthwhile to say."

Journal Entry, May 18

I kind of blew it. Again.
Told Bishop Crandall
to put his advice where
his toilet paper sticks.

Bad move. I knew it
when I said it, but oh well.
I just don't care anymore.
About anything.

Mom actually cried
and sent me to my
room. I left the door
open so I could hear.

Bishop Crandall said
I should be punished.
Severely. "My children
get the belt," he hinted.

I don't know what kind
of bomb Mom and Dad
will drop, or when they'll
drop it. But I do know

if Dad comes at me
with a belt,
I'm gone.
For good.

That is, if there's
any of me left.

Dad Dropped the Bomb

Five days later.
Three bombs, actually.

Being so self-absorbed
for so many weeks,

I guess I never noticed
the too familiar signs.

Mom had been tired lately.
Throwing up a lot.

> *Your mother is pregnant.*
> *Ultrasound says it's a boy.*

Boom! Boom! A baby.
And a son. Finally, a son.

> *Too much stress could*
> *hurt your mother or Samuel.*

They'd already picked a name?
Too much stress, meaning me?

> *We've decided to send you*
> *away for the summer.*

Ka-boom! Away? Where
could they send me?

> *You'll be staying out on*
> *your Aunt Jeanette's ranch.*

Aunt Jeanette? The sister he'd barely
spoken to in over thirty years?

> *No trouble out there but snakes*
> *and empty mine shafts.*

"I thought you couldn't
stand Aunt Jeanette."

> *She and I don't see eye to*
> *eye on every little thing. . . .*

Why then? Why exile me
to the wilds of eastern Nevada?

> *But your mother and I want you out*
> *of here, and Jeanette was the only*
> *one who would take you.*

I Didn't Want to Go

But they played the guilt card,
which gave me no choice. I did feel

guilty

about lying to get my way,

guilty

about almost giving my virginity away
to someone who didn't deserve it,

guilty

about the things we'd done instead,

guiltier

about broken windows, broken noses.
And should I somehow make Mom

lose

her baby, I would forever

lose

every inch of self-respect,

lose

every ounce of my newfound belief
that I wasn't born to be a

loser.

So I agreed to a road trip across Foreverland.
With my dad at the wheel.

East from Carson City

The road stretched long and longer toward
yesterday, sculpted in distant granite hills
and splintered ghost town boardwalks.

The Subaru's tires whined along the asphalt,
a stray gray thread in the khaki weave—sage
and hardpan, cheatgrass and bitterbrush.

Mirage puddles emptied, one into the next,
and I wanted to dissolve, pour myself
on the pavement and ride along. Somewhere.
Anywhere but where I was going.

Across salt flats, we picked up speed, past
giant knolls of shifting sand and travel-trailer tenements,
where rusting semis cohabited with Silver Stream
wannabes and a couple of lone tepees.

I wanted Dad to slow down, so I might
catch a glimpse of what might live there,
where civilization ended
and my new life was about to begin.

Beneath a sag of barbed wire was a stiff
bluetick hound. A ratty black Lab mourned him,

from far enough to weather flies, but close

enough to chase away bone pickers,
flying lazy eights in the blue desert sky,
searching for the carcass du jour.

Did anyone miss those dogs?
Would anyone miss me?

So I Ventured

"Will you miss me, Dad?"

> Now, you have to remember
> that my dad and I hardly shared
> fifty words in any given day.
> I'd just used up one tenth of my allotment.

> > *Miss you? I don't even*
> > *know you, Pattyn.*

> His admission stung. Enough
> to stick a big ol' lump in my throat.
> Enough to give me the courage
> to ask, around the lump,

"Whose fault is that?"

> His hands tensed on the wheel
> and I could see the little veins
> at his temples swell and pump faster.
> Too much to think about?

> > *Enough blame to go*
> > *around, I guess.*

He wanted to let it drop.
I wasn't about to give him his way.
He could blame me for many things.
But not for the closeness we'd lost.

So I Argued

"No way, Dad. I'm not taking
the blame here. Yes, I've done
some things lately I'm not exactly
proud of. But the distance between us?
Don't you dare point your finger at me.

"You work, eat dinner, watch TV.
Sometimes you'll play with the little
ones, but you never talk to me.
All I've ever wanted is your respect.
But you don't even know I exist."

There! A quality dialogue.
Only it was mostly a monologue.
Dad mulled it over. Nodded once
or twice at the conversation going on
inside his head. Then he said,

Respect is a two-way street.
Do you respect me?
My house?
My rules?

I loved Dad, despite everything,
wanted more than anything

for him to love me back.
I respected him once.
But what about now?

"How can I respect a house
where women are no more than
servants? How can I respect rules
laid down by a phantom father?
How can I respect a man who . . ."

I didn't dare say it, did I?

Who what?

"Who spends all day . . ."

Go ahead.

"Who h . . ."

Spit it out.

"Oh, never mind."

End of conversation.

Halfway

Across the wide state of Nevada,
the country changed from sage flats
to piñon- and juniper-covered mountains.

Some two hundred north-south ranges
dissect this arid land, making Nevada
the most mountainous state in the Union.

One after one, they rose and fell,
and as I watched, the horizon
seemed to breathe. It was eerie.

And beautiful. A perfect backdrop
for silence.

We stopped for lunch in Ely (Ee-lee,
not Ee-lie—better pronounce
things right in eastern Nevada).

Ely isn't a whole lot different
than in the cowboy days except
for fast food, faster cars, and espresso bars.

Dad had grown up on a ranch,
some fifteen miles south of town.
"Do you ever miss it?" I asked.

Around bites of Burger King,
he admitted, *I miss the quiet.*

I miss seeing from here to forever.
I miss how people mind their own
business, but still can be counted on.

That Was the Closest to Human

I'd seen Dad in a real long time.
    A bolt of pain seared my heart.
        Why couldn't I know my dad
            as this almost vulnerable man?
                Was this the person Mom fell for?

We turned south out of Ely,
    drove parallel to the most gorgeous
        mountain range east of the Sierra.
            I pictured Dad, as a boy, bouncing
                along in a pickup on his way to school.

Grandma Jane had to drive him
    into town. Grandpa Paul couldn't
        work a clutch with only one leg.
            I remembered these stories from
                that distant time when Dad still spoke.

He didn't speak much on the two-hour
    drive to Caliente. I wondered
        if he was lost in some childhood
            reverie, or had simply closed up
                again, like an oyster around its pearl.

We Hit Caliente Around Four

As towns went, it wasn't much—
a trailer park, a couple of motels,
a restaurant or two, a tavern,
and a hardware store, which carried
shoes and a few stitches of clothing.

Smallish houses sat in neat little rows,
defending a little park, two churches,
and the Mormon stake house—
the fanciest building in town.
On the outskirts was a roping arena.

Dad made me sit in the car
while he ran into a little market.
He bought flowers for Aunt Jeanette,
a soda for me and, I'm pretty
sure, a bottle of Johnnie WB.

As I waited, a Union Pacific roared
by. The tracks in Caliente are a major
thoroughfare for freight trains,
moving goods north to south
and, of course, back again.

The windows rattled till I thought
they just might shatter. I considered
catching a lapful of glass,
as a shiny blue pickup parked
in the adjoining space.

A guy climbed out, and he was to die
for. Who knew they made them
so killer cute, out there in the sticks?
He noticed me noticing him
and flashed a smile that could melt lead.

Furnace Lips strutted toward the store,
turned at the door, and gave me another
solid once-over. It was my first hint
that life out there in Nowhereville
might not be so bad after all.

Aunt Jeanette Lived

Several miles
out of town,
way back
up a wide ravine.

We paralleled the train
tracks past lush
pastureland,
verdant meadows,
shady ranches,
and the most
awesome rock
formations
I'd ever seen.

The farther
we drove,
the more
I fell in love
with rural Nevada's
raw beauty.
No neon.
No walls.
No traffic.
No row after row

of identical cracker-
box houses.
This wasn't punishment.
It was freedom.

I'm Not Sure Why

I knew that then.
Call it

            intuition.

Whatever it was,
my mind

            swayed

from fear and
uncertainty;

            my heart

veered from hurt
and bitterness

            toward

the unlikely idea
that, away from
home, my

            future

might
blossom with

            hope.

Aunt Jeanette's Ranch

Was 160 water-fed acres—lush, untamed.
We pulled into her cottonwood-shaded

driveway. A mule brayed and two tricolored
dogs came to greet us, tail stumps wagging.

Next came a parade of cats, all colors,
all sizes. Strangers demanded investigation.

Even the geese had to check us out.
A nasty gander approached, hissing.
                Aunt Jeanette appeared suddenly.
                You scat on outta here, Grady Goose!
The gander scrambled out of sight,
protesting loudly the entire way.
                Aunt Jeanette gave me a once-over.
                Damn, girl, you have grown.
We'd last seen each other six
Christmases ago, at Grandpa Paul's.
                It's about time you came for a visit.
                This ol' place can get pretty lonely.
No doubt, with no company but animals.
"How have you been, Aunt Jeanette?"
                Call me Aunt J. Keep saying "Aunt
                Jeanette," we'll be here all day.

I smiled. "Okay, then, Aunt J."
Dad grunted something like hello.

> *Welcome, Stephen. Let's all go inside.*
> *Supper will be ready 'fore you know it.*

I really can't stay, Dad tried
to say. *Janice is expecting me.*

> *Too late to start back now. Call your wife,*
> *tell her you'll be home tomorrow.*

A woman who took no crap from Dad?
She and I would get along just fine.

We Followed Her Inside

Dad carried my single suitcase,
stuffed to the brim with homemade clothes.
I carried my backpack, stuffed to the brim
with begged and borrowed books.

>Aunt J kept a clipped, measured
>pace. I watched the hitch of her narrow
>hips, the swish of her single, long braid,
>bronze shot through with silver.

>>In her day, she must have been very
>>beautiful. She had married once,
>>but I'd never heard details, only
>>that her husband, Stan, had died.

The outside of the long, low house
wore a fresh coat of white, with a pale
blue colonnade and shutters to add
a bit of color to the tidy porch.

>Inside, simple antique furniture graced
>polished hardwood floors. Wreaths and quilts
>and afghans brightened every room.
>I saw no photographs at all.

One wall of the living room housed
a gun cabinet, filled with deadly treasures.
Aunt Jeanette was a cross between
Annie Oakley and Martha Stewart!

At Dinner

Dad was outnumbered
gender-wise, and

                              hurting

for a snort. It was easy
to see Aunt J made him

                              uncomfortable

but I had no clear idea why.
I only knew some past

                              upset

had kept them from speaking
for a good long while.

                              Insane,

I thought, not talking to your
sibling for decades. So,

                              crazy

me, I asked, "Are you two
still mad at each other?"

                              Incensed,

        Dad answered, *Who said we*
        were mad at each other?

                              Incredulous,

Aunt J contradicted,
Best let water passed
under the bridge keep
on trickling downstream.

Journal Entry, May 27

I'm supposed to be asleep, but
Dad and Aunt J are talking,
and I'm eavesdropping big-
time. Dad's slurring, so he
must have stepped outside
for a good ol' dose of Johnnie.
Wonder what Aunt J thinks
about his un-Mormon breath.

He keeps telling her not to cut
me slack and she keeps telling
him it's her place, she'll do as
she pleases, and he can just
take me on home if that's how
he feels. Funny, but I don't
think I want to go home.
Unlike yesterday.

I don't know what life here
will be like, but Dad made it
clear life back home would
be hell, and I sure believe that.
He won't even miss me.
I doubt anyone will miss me.

Except maybe Jackie, when
she gets back from camp.

The creepy thing is, I won't
miss them, either. How can
you go through sixteen years
with your family and not miss
them when you leave?
What's wrong with my family?
What's wrong with me?

Dad Motored Off

Very early the next morning.
      I was sawing major ZZZZs.
He didn't bother with good-byes,
      which only hurt a little.

Aunt J let me sleep in. I woke all
      alone in a strange room with chintz
curtains and dried flower wreaths
      on bright turquoise walls.

The only sound was the *tick-tick*
      of an iris-shaped clock and,
somewhere outside, Aunt J's pleasant
      song as she puttered around the yard.

I didn't move for several minutes,
      just lay there, contemplating.
What was expected of me here?
      No one had mentioned a thing.

Sacrament services were obviously
      not high on the list. At home,
I'd be sweating and suffering
      Bishop Crandall's evil stare.

No diapers here. No kids to tend.
        Dishes for two were nothing.
Was I supposed to plant a garden?
        Feed the livestock? Count cats?

I got up and went to the window.
        Outside, a small breeze toyed
with a wind chime and ruffled
        Aunt J's small patch of grass.

I remembered Dad's words:
        No trouble there but rattlesnakes
and deserted mine shafts.
        I was beginning to believe it.

The First Week or So

Aunt J and I sort of poked
at each other, testing
the water, as they say.

She talked about life
in the sticks.

I talked about life
in the suburbs.

She talked about
solitary living.

I talked about
overcrowding.

She talked about the joy—
and pain—of physical labor.

I talked about diapers
and dishpan hands.

She talked about dogs, cats,
horses, and mules.

I talked about jackrabbits
and pesky little sisters.

She talked about hot
summers and hard winters.

I talked about school—up
until the last few months.

Which finally led her to ask,
*Do you want to talk about
why you're here?*

I Did—and I Didn't

I liked Aunt J—her soft-spoken
way, her honesty. But I didn't
feel secure with her yet.

> How far could I trust her?
> How much did she know?
> How much did she want to know?

So I probed, "Why
do you think I'm here?
What did Dad tell you?"

> She sat quietly for a minute.
> *He said there was trouble
> at school, trouble with a boy. . . .*

I nodded. "A little
trouble with both,
okay? Is that all?"

> She looked me in the eye.
> *He said your bishop has decided
> you're possessed by Satan.*

I snorted. "Because
I want a normal life
and someone to love me?"

> *Is breaking someone's nose
> normal, Pattyn? Do you think
> your young man loved you?*

Okay. Valid questions.
"No, he didn't love me,
and that made me . . ."

Angry? Enough to make
you lose your temper and hit
someone else in the face?

"Hurt. Enough to want
to make someone else
hurt too. I'm so sorry."

If you know why it happened,
and you're truly sorry,
I doubt you're possessed.

"I'm not possessed,
Aunt Jeanette, and I'm glad
you don't think so either."

Satan has bigger fish to fry,
mostly in Washington, D.C.
Now how about dinner?

Next Day, I Found Out

Aunt J had no expectations
regarding my doing chores.
>   *You're a guest. 'Course, if you want*
>   *to pitch in, I'm not sayin' no.*
What else did I have to do?
Besides read, that is.
>   *Got a big patch of weeds needs pullin'.*
>   *And you can toss chicken scratch.*
Pullin' and tossin'. No problem.
Mindless labor, easily done.
>   *I do have a big project on tap for some*
>   *time in the next week or two.*
Big project? Like digging
a pond or raising a barn?
>   *I've got to move a hundred head of cattle.*
>   *You ever ridden a horse before?*
I did a pony ride once. Round
and round in a little circle.
>   *Old Poncho doesn't ask for much.*
>   *All you have to do is stay in the saddle.*
I figured I could manage that.
How hard could it be?

Aunt J Figured

I'd better practice a little.
Old Poncho stood like a champ
while she tossed the saddle
over his slightly swayed back.

> *See, you reach under his belly,*
> *grab the cinch, put it through*
> *this ring, and pull tight.*

Poncho gave a little *oomph*,
but didn't really complain.
I stroked his nose, watched
his whiskers twitch.

> *Now put your left foot into*
> *the left stirrup and pull*
> *yourself right on up there.*

Except for a tense second
or two as my pants stretched
quite tightly at the rear, I
climbed on with relative ease.

> *Squeeze with your knees,*
> *keep your heels dropped,*
> *hands gentle on the reins.*

Knees, heels, and hands
in approximate position,
I clucked my tongue to make
him go. Poncho was deaf!

He's not deaf, only stubborn.
Give him a little nudge
with your heels.

That worked and walking
was easy, like straddling
a well-worn rocking chair,
plod-ka-plod-ka-plod.

That's it. Pull the reins
right to turn that way.
Pull 'em left to go left.

Poncho performed as
requested and I felt just
like a cowgirl. Until
he started to trot.

You're gonna get whiplash,
bouncing like that. Squeeze
those knees harder.

I tried, but nothing I did could
keep my butt in the saddle.
Poncho responded by trotting
faster. *Plop-plop-plop-plop-plop.*

Aunt J dissolved into
deviant laughter.
Make him stop.

"Whoa!" I hollered, much
to Poncho's amusement.
I pulled back on the reins.
Too much slack.

> *Tighten your grip*
> *and yank hard!*
> Aunt J shouted.

I yanked. Poncho stopped.
The final bounce planted
my behind in the saddle,
bruising my bruises.

> *Looks like you'll*
> *have to work on*
> *that trot!*

*J*ournal Entry, June 6

I rode a horse today!
I've never been sorer
in my whole entire life!
I think my butt is majorly
black and blue. (I can't
really see it in the mirror.)

So why am I so proud of myself?

Aunt J said she's proud of me
too, even if my trot does need
a little work. She's proud of me!
I can't believe she and Dad
are related.

We're going to move her
longhorns from low pasture
to high meadow. Some ranchers
use ATVs or even helicopters
to move their cattle.
Aunt J uses horses and dogs.
Just like in the movies.

I wonder if movie cowboys
ever got sore butts.
I wonder if horseback riding
can give me a shapely butt.
I wonder if I'll ever learn
to ride a horse.

I wonder how Mom is feeling.
I wonder if Jackie liked camp.
I wonder if Georgia has stopped
sucking her thumb.
I wonder if Derek and Carmen
are still together.
(I wonder if Carmen is pregnant yet.)
I wonder if Dad misses me at all.

The Next Morning

I came downstairs to the aroma
of coffee. Really strong coffee.
                       It smelled delicious.
Aunt J sipped a cup, offered one
to me. I shook my head. "No, thanks."
                       It was a sin.
Considering my recent behavior,
I wasn't sure why coffee worried me.
                       It was tempting.
Aunt J said it was up to me, but far
as she knew, God couldn't care less.
                       It made my mouth water.
Was it the smell? The idea of giving
in to temptation? I hadn't a clue.
                       It was wrong, and I knew it.
Whatever it was, I crumbled like
biscotti, in need of black coffee.
                       It demanded I try it.
A small sip wrinkled my nose.
A big gulp went down like water.
                       It was bitter.
Aunt J offered sugar and cream,
but I wanted the truth of coffee.
                       It was the best thing I'd ever tasted.

What Had Happened to Me

Beer. Tequila. Coffee.
   Heavy petting, which,
      I had to admit, I enjoyed.
         What was next? Excommunication?

What if it was? Could I
    deal with that? Could my
       family? Would they all
         be considered outcasts?

Would they hate me
    if they were? Dumb
       question, right? So, okay,
        if they disowned me,

like Dad had disowned
    Douglas, would I get
       over it, create a solid
         existence without them?

Would I find a way
    to forgive myself, even
       love myself, or would
         I react like Molly

           and end the pain completely?

After Breakfast

I asked Aunt J if I could borrow
a rifle for a little target practice.

> *Sure. Why not? They're wasting*
> *away in that cabinet.*

Wasting away? "How come?
You must like to shoot."

> *I do hunt venison once a year.*
> *I don't especially enjoy it.*

So much for Annie Oakley.
"Why do you have so many guns?"

> *Stan collected them, more for show*
> *than use. Extravagant, really.*

But they were beautiful.
"What do you mean?"

> *A person only needs three guns—*
> *a good hunting rifle . . .*

For filling the freezer
with venison once a year . . .

> *a handgun for protection, and*
> *a scattergun—for varmints.*

I had no urge to mess with shotguns.
A big one could take your arm off.

> *You're welcome to borrow whatever.*
> *Take the pickup and make a day of it.*

Was she crazy? "Uh, thanks, Aunt
J, but I don't know how to drive."
                    What? Going on seventeen and
                    you still can't drive?
"Dad said if my husband wants me
to know how, he'll have to teach me."

The Look on Her Face

Was priceless. I'd definitely hit
some kind of a nerve. Aunt J
gave me a nudge toward the door.

Let's go.

An old Ford pickup, circa 1950-
something, loitered in the scattered
shade of the driveway.

Get in. I'll teach you.

I glanced at the classic truck,
with bug-eyed headlights above a big
grill and not a ding under the primer.

Don't worry. You can't hurt her.

I doubted that. But the freedom
Aunt J had offered me
was a powerful temptation.

Get in. We'll be fine.

I slid under the steering
wheel, hands shaky as Jell-O.
Had no idea what to do next.

Put the key in the ignition.

In it went, like it wanted to
be there. One turn and the motor
sputtered to life.

Right pedal, go. Left pedal, stop.

I punched the right pedal.
The engine revved and roared
a protest. Aunt J grinned.

First you have to put it in gear . . .

Duh! The gearshift.
How many times had I
watched someone use it?

Right now she's in Park.

Oh yeah. *P* for park,
R for reverse . . . "So what
does *D* stand for?"

Drive.

And before I knew it, I was.

We Started Down

A wide dirt track that paralleled the fence line,
that paralleled the main road in from town.

Steering came easy enough. Turn the wheel,
not too hard, and go the direction you turned it.

The gas pedal wasn't a mystery either. Push
harder, go faster. Let up on it, slow down.

The brakes took a bit of getting used to. Push
the pedal easy, slow gently. Stomp? Don't!

After a couple of steering over-corrections and a
herky-jerky start or two, I began to get the hang of it.

I was bumping along, thoroughly engrossed in driving
a straight line, when Aunt J interrupted. *Stop a sec.*

Another pickup, a blue Dodge Dakota, had pulled
onto the shoulder on the far side of the fence.

I braked the Ford to a quick stop, as the Dodge's driver
stood up from changing his flat. *Morning, Ms. Petrie.*

Furnace Lips! That killer cute guy knew Aunt J?
Apparently, she knew him, too. *Hello, Ethan. Everything okay?*

It is now, he said, flashing that familiar smile. *Next time,
back to Firestones. These Michelins can't take a finishing nail.*

Aunt J chuckled, then gestured in my direction. *I'd like you
to meet my niece Pattyn. She's visiting me for the summer.*

Pleased to make your acquaintance, Pattyn. His eyes,
filled with assessment, drew level with mine. *Pretty name.*

I nodded, afraid my voice might stick to my tongue. Aunt
J saved me major embarrassment. *How's your father coping?*

Ethan's smile dried up like a summer mud puddle.
He's okay, I guess. But she left a pretty big hole.

I know she did, Ethan, soothed Aunt J. *Let me know
if you need anything at all, and give your dad my best.*

We Drove Off in Opposite Directions

Ethan's big Dodge cruised smoothly
south on the asphalt, while Aunt J's
old Ford stuttered north in the dirt,
with me, Pattyn (pretty name!),
behind the wheel.

Aunt J stared out the window, mired in
some daydream. Where her mind
had wandered, I couldn't say.
Anyway, my own mind was
glued on Ethan.

How did he and Aunt J know each other?
Who was the woman whose memory
snatched away his incredible
smile? Could someone like
me give it back?

Aunt J knew most of those answers,
of course. But I sensed she wasn't
in the mood to discuss them. And
I wasn't quite ready to admit
my budding infatuation.

I found a big, wide turnaround place,
did an about-face, and putted back
to the ranch house, still stuck
on Ethan and how I might
get to know him.

Turned out it wasn't hard at all.

Journal Entry, June 7

Yesterday I thought riding a horse
was an accomplishment. Today
I learned how to drive. I think
I did pretty good, too. At least,
I didn't run into anything or
blow up Aunt J's pickup.

It wasn't exactly legal, I know.
But Aunt J said it was her property,
she'd damn well do as she pleased,
and, besides, some laws were meant
to be broken—laws made for no
reason but to keep good people in check.
She said the government was like an
impatient cowboy—quick to hobble
a spirited horse until it wasn't good
for anything but dog food.

I also met Ethan today. He is by
far the most beautiful man I've
ever seen. Aunt J said he's a college
sophomore, which must mean
he goes to college. I wonder where.
No "institutes of higher learning"
out here in the sticks, I'll bet.

*I wonder why I'm wondering
about him at all. He's so out of my
league. Ah, who cares? At least
he's giving me something to think
about besides the mess I left
behind in Carson City.*

*I've been here eleven days, and they
haven't called once to check up
on me, or even just to say hi.
Won't Dad croak when he finds
out Aunt J taught me to drive?
He'll have to lock up his keys.*

If he ever lets me come home.

On Saturday

After breakfast and chores, Aunt J said she needed to
   run into Panaca to pick up supplies from the feed store.
   She tossed me the keys. *You drive. Practice makes perfect.*
It was my first time on an honest-to-goodness road.

Aunt J played with the radio, looking for country tunes.
   She barely even flinched the time or two I miscalculated,
   spinning the tires up the dirt shoulder, then back to asphalt.
The second time, I said, "Okay, that had to scare you."

She quit fiddling with knobs and looked over.
   I've made it through some god-awful things, Pattyn.
   Nothing much can scare me. No sir, not anymore.
She opened the window wide, inviting the wind.

I'd connected with Aunt J in a special way, yet how
   little I knew about her. She had trusted me with her
   truck. Would she trust me enough to confide secrets?
"What awful things, Aunt J? Tell me, please."

I didn't dare take my eyes off the road, but I felt
   her withdrawal into that distant place deep inside.
   We bumped along for several silent minutes, as she
settled into the indefinable space where she needed to be.

And if we hadn't crossed the railroad tracks,
    signaling the highway's imminent approach, she might
    have broken down and told me everything right then.
Instead she said, *I'd better drive from here.*

I pulled over, remembered to push the gearshift
    into *P* for park. Aunt J came around and took the wheel,
    and as I scooted my black-and-blue butt across the seat,
I vowed to weasel her secrets, however dark they might be.

At the Feed Store

I followed Aunt J inside,
letting my eyes adjust to filtered light
and my nose admire the potpourri.

Leather.
Grain.
Alfalfa.

Aunt J disappeared out back
while I wandered over to a far wall,
drawn by a riot of sound.

Cheeps.
Scuffs.
Hisses.

Yellow fluffs under warming
lamps, sifting through scratch
and testing stumpy wings.

Chicks.
Ducklings.
Goslings.

Finally, I heard Aunt J. I turned
to see her talking to a guy
with a vaguely familiar voice.

Tall.
Built.
Gorgeous.

Gorgeous? Ethan! And I hadn't
even brushed my hair! I hurried
outside, hoping he wouldn't see me.

Ha.
Ha.
Ha.

He Trailed Aunt J

To the pickup, carrying a fifty-pound sack
of cracked corn like burlap-wrapped feathers,
tossed it in the bed, went back for another.

I dropped my face, so he wouldn't notice
its ordinariness as he passed the window.

I'm pretty sure he glanced my way once
or twice, walking by. Striding by, with long,
lean legs, hugged tight by Wranglers.

I pretended not to watch, but the corner
of my eye caught every little detail.

The way he moved. How his muscles flexed.
Facial structure. The vivid green of his eyes
beneath a long wave of hair, mink brown.

Justin and Derek could eat their hearts out—
if Tiffany and Carmen didn't beat them to it.

Three sacks of grain and a bag of dog food
later, he thanked Aunt J and started off.
At the door he turned, and I just about died

when he flashed me his should-be-famous
smile and mouthed, *See you soon.*

See Me Soon?

What did he mean by that?

Considering recent events,

I was going to stay innocent.

I was going to die celibate.

I would not date again.

I would not marry, ever.

No man would own me.

despite all of the above,

so suddenly and completely

Did I care?

I shouldn't care.

Men were evil.

Men were trouble.

Men lied.

Men cheated.

So why,

was I,

fascinated with *this* man?

Aunt J Knew, Too

Cute did not define it. "I guess.
Who is he, anyway?"

He's cute, huh?

*Ethan is the son
of an old friend.*

Ah. Things were getting clearer.
But . . . "His mom or his dad?"

Both, but mostly his dad.

We were almost on a roll.
"So, um . . . he lives around here?"

Just outside of Caliente.

We lived just outside of Caliente.
"Near the ranch?"

Right down the road. Why?

Why, indeed? "No special reason
except he said he'd see me soon."

*He will. He's helping us
move the cattle.*

Oh brother. I felt like a total
dolt. "Oh, okay."

*I figured someone with
experience couldn't hurt.*

Someone without a bruised butt,
she meant. "Probably not."

Especially someone cute.

Was she playing matchmaker?
I smiled. "When's he coming?"

Next Sunday. It's his day off.

Next Sunday? Eight whole days
away? "Not tomorrow?"

He and his dad have plans.

I decided to fish a little. "Don't you
ever go to sacrament meetings?"

Not this ol' bird.
You're free to go.

Free not to go was more accurate.
"But you're Mormon, aren't you?"

Was once. Gave up
on it, though.

The ice had been broken—chipped,
anyway. "How come?"

Long story, one you
maybe shouldn't hear.

One I had to hear, now. "I want to
know, Aunt J. Need to know."

Maybe after supper.
I have to unload the feed.

It Seemed Like Forever

But after dinner, we settled
into chairs on the porch.
The dogs parked at our feet,
and cats rubbed up into our laps
as Aunt J spilled her tale.

> *You might think I've never been in love,*
> *but you'd be wrong. I was seventeen,*
> *Kevin was eighteen. And he wasn't Mormon.*
> *I was so much like you, Pattyn.*
> *Full of life, full of hope.*
> *And I fell desperately in love*
> *with a man neither my family*
> *nor my church would ever accept.*

Intergenerational déjà vu?
My stomach churned.

> *I kept right on seeing him anyway.*
> *We planned to marry, just as soon*
> *as I graduated high school. He even*
> *wanted me to go to college. Said any*
> *girl as smart as I was should have a calling*
> *other than kids. We were only kids ourselves,*
> *of course, and like most kids that age,*
> *our love moved way beyond kissing.*

No wonder she'd hesitated
to come clean.

Ely was—and still is—a very small town.
Word got around till it reached your grandfather.
He forbade me to see Kevin, but love
was more powerful than fear. I was just
five months shy of my eighteenth birthday
when your father caught Kevin and me
parked near Burnside Lake. Stephen
pointed a .45 right between Kevin's eyes
and ordered us to get out of the car.

The picture rolled clearly
into view.

He made us both kneel in the dirt.
The pistol swung my way. "Father sent
a message," he said. "You are not to see
this man again, or both of you will die."
I started to cry and Kevin reached for me.
Stephen cocked the hammer. "Don't
touch her or I swear I'll shoot you dead."
Stephen was home after his first tour
in Vietnam. He'd done plenty of killing.
We had no reason to doubt he'd do more.

I didn't doubt it either.
"What did you do?"

I begged Stephen to leave us alone. Asked
how he'd feel if Father demanded he leave

Molly. He laughed and told me to get in
his car. When I refused, he put the gun
barrel against my cheek, pulled it gently
toward my temple. "I'll use this," he said.
"One more would mean nothing." A crazy
fire flickered in his eyes. I believed, then as
now, he could have killed me as easily
as he slaughtered innocent Vietnamese.

And have yet another
ghost to haunt him.

I stood and started for his car, afraid for
my life, for Kevin's life. I heard Stephen
tell Kevin, "If you ever so much as glance
at my sister again, I will hunt you down
like a dirty coyote." Then he brought
that .45 hard against Kevin's jaw. Cracked
it wide open, but that wasn't enough. Stephen
beat that man till I thought a bullet would've
been kinder. So now you know why Stephen
and I didn't speak for so many years.

One piece of the puzzle.
"But what about the church?"

Stephen damn near laid Kevin in his grave.
But when Kevin tried to press charges, Sheriff
Steele claimed there wasn't enough evidence.

See, he was also our bishop at the time. Church law before any other, you know that. I suffered his "court of love," admitting as few dirty details as they'd allow. When I turned eighteen, I did go off to college. And I never sat through another Sunday from hell. Kevin moved away.
I kept hoping he'd write. He never did.

I Was Stunned

I mean, I knew my dad could be
        cruel, but this went way beyond
anything I'd ever witnessed.

        After a few shocked moments,
I got up, went over and put my arms
        around Aunt J's neck. "I'm sorry."

She tensed, as if she'd never been
        hugged before. Then her shoulders
sagged. *It was a long time ago.*

        I came around and sat at her feet.
So much sadness in her eyes!
        Why hadn't I noticed it before?

"Did you ever see Kevin again?"
        She nodded. *But by then it was too
late. I'd already married Stan.*

        "But you did fall in love again, didn't
you? With Stan?" You had to fall
        in love to get married. Didn't you?

Aunt J stared toward the hills,
        crimson in sunset. *Real love*
finds you once, if you're lucky.

        "But what about . . . ," I started
to say. There was so much
        more I wanted to know.

Some people never find love at all,
        Pattyn. Count yourself blessed
if it ever happens your way.

We Went Inside

To our separate rooms,
where the walls formed
boxes around us. And I
wondered what Aunt J
was doing, alone in her
own private cubicle.

Was she crying over
Kevin? Cursing Dad?
Had she tucked it all
back away into that
terrible space where
nightmares are born?

Closed in by plaster,
question after question
infiltrated my aching
head. What about Stan?
Hadn't Aunt J loved
him at least a little?

How could a sheriff
swear to uphold the law
when his allegiance lay
elsewhere? How could
Grandpa Paul send Dad
on an armed mission?

Would Dad really have
pulled that trigger, killed
his sister and Kevin, just
because they were in love?
The obvious answer kept
me awake half the night.

*J*ournal Entry, June 10

I learned some terrible things
today—all about Aunt J and
her "forever love," Kevin.
It seems my wonderful father
drove them apart. With a gun.
Maybe that shouldn't surprise
me. But it does.

How many more miserable
things has Dad done,
things I'll never know about
and don't really want to?
How does he dare judge me?

I want Aunt J not to be lonely.
I want her to find another love,
but she says we only get one
real love, and only if we're lucky.
Will I be lucky? If I am, will
someone drive him away?
Someone like Dad?

Someone
like
me?

I Thought About Ethan a Lot

Over the next few days.
Weird, I know, that

              someone

you've never met could
thaw the ice damming inside,

              warm

you like a summer morning,
even though he's not yours

              to hold.

I thought of Aunt J, the love
of her life dissolved into

              dreams.

Did she hurt every day? Or
had she locked away all

              memories

of him, condemned them
to that muddy well only

              drawn from

in times of strangling
loneliness? Would I find

              forever

love? Did I really want to,
when forever was a word

              without meaning?

Tuesday Evening

Aunt J and
I planted ourselves on the porch
to watch the
stars poke out, twinkle by twinkle,
in the slate
blue sky.
It was a
nightly affair, and one no city
dweller
could ever take notice of, amidst
sodium and
neon lights.

Cutting
through the blossoming darkness,
headlights
appeared on the road, slowed,
turned into
the driveway.
Ethan
shimmied down from the pickup
cab, shiny
even under the muted glow of
gathering
moonlight.

Evening,
ladies. Just thought I'd drop by
on my way
home with that new pair of reins.
Came in
today.   *Thank you,*
Mr. Carter, said Aunt J. *Sit on down*
and stay
awhile. We haven't had dessert yet.
Homemade
strawberry pie.

He did just
that. We spent the next hour or so
immersed in
lighthearted conversation, strawberries,
and whipped
cream.

After He Left

Aunt J noted, *I think he's*
taken with you, girl.

Taken with me? "No way.
Why would he be?"

She shrugged. *He could have*
brought the reins on Sunday.

Which proved exactly zip.
He was driving by . . .

Even if the reins were important,
he didn't have to stay for dessert.

"Maybe not. But I'm not
good enough for him."

Why would you say such
a thing, Pattyn?

"Have you looked at him,
Aunt J? He's beautiful."

Have you looked in a mirror
lately? So are you. So are you.

"Me? Beautiful? I'm
plain as cardboard."

That may be how you see yourself,
but the rest of the world would
be hard put to agree. You shine
brighter than the Milky Way.

*Now there are those who might
try to take that from you, but
you don't have to give it away.
Keep on shining, Pattyn.*

*And when the right young man
comes along, he'll love you all
the more for giftin' this sad
planet with your light.*

I Didn't Know

How to respond,
but with a simple
thank you. Then
I excused myself
and went in to bed.

I sat in the rocker,
staring out at a corner
of the Milky Way,
Aunt J's words
floating in my head.

I'd never thought
of myself as any-
thing but banal.
Could I see myself
as beautiful instead?

Smaller steps, maybe?
"Pretty" would do, or
even "cute." Still,
this was territory I
almost feared to tread.

I felt like a snake,
perhaps a bit afraid
of the brand-new
serpent, commanding
an old skin to shed.

The Morning After

Found me antsy, so I borrowed
        Aunt J's .22 and hiked back up
                into the summer-kissed hills.

Before I left, she insisted I clean
        the rifle, which had sat, unused, for
                more years than she could remember.

I'd never cleaned a gun before, and
        as I thought about it, I began to wonder
                why Dad had never taught me the skill.

A dirty gun is no kind of weapon,
        Aunt J said. *You could take out*
                an eye as easily as hit a target.

Anyway, she showed me how,
        and as I walked, the scent of gun oil
                blended with evergreen. Heavenly!

It had been several weeks since
        I'd shot a gun and for ten or fifteen
                minutes I felt as rusty as tin in salt air.

But then it all came tumbling back
and for quite some time I amused myself,
shooting ever-smaller pinecones from the trees.

As I wandered farther and farther
into the belly of the forest, a flash
of beige brushed the corner of my eye.

I froze, and so did the doe, heavy with
fawn. We gave each other a stout once-over,
then she flinched and vanished, a whisper.

It came to me that I never considered
raising that gun and taking aim, not that
a .22 was much in the way of a venison rifle.

And in a moment of clarity, I understood
that while killing for meat can be tolerated,
killing for passion might very well be easier.

By Friday Afternoon

I decided my bottom had healed
enough to practice a bit on Old
Poncho. I didn't want to look like
a complete fool in front of Ethan.
                (The best-laid plans . . .)
Aunt J was taking a nap when I
wandered down to the barn,
clipped a rope to Poncho's halter,
and led him to the tack room.
                (That much I remembered.)
I slipped a blanket over his back,
topped it with the saddle, reached
for the cinch. That's when things
got a bit hazy memory-wise.
                (I'd only seen it done once!)
Through one ring, pull it tight,
now some kind of a knot?
Okay, it didn't feel exactly right,
but I calculated it might do.
                (Math was not my best subject.)
Whatever I did, it managed
to hold my weight as I stepped
up into the stirrup and pulled
myself into the saddle.
                (Thereby increasing my confidence.)

I'd forgotten the bridle completely,
but Poncho didn't seem to care.
He steered just fine without a bit,
at least while circling at a walk.
                    (Building my confidence even more.)
I knew I had to trot sometime,
master whatever technique
stopped one from bouncing.
I nudged him to pick up speed.
                    (Things started to go wrong immediately.)
Plop-plop-plop. Bounce, bounce,
bounce. Maybe faster was better?
I kicked once. Poncho upped his pace.
Still bouncing, I kicked again.
                    (In retrospect, it was a bad move.)
Poncho had had quite enough.
He feinted right. I leaned right,
just as he shifted left. Completely
baffled, my body kept right.
                    (About then, I suspected something was amiss.)
The saddle moved along with
my weight, cocking sideways.
I grabbed the horn and planted
my feet in the stirrups.
                    (Not exactly the right thing to do.)

Poncho put on the brakes,
resulting in the saddle and me
coming to a sudden halt, at a
ninety-degree angle to the horizon.
            (Hilarious, if it had been someone else.)
About then, I happened to glance
toward the driveway, where a shiny
blue Dodge Dakota had parked.
Ethan stood beside it, grinning.
            (Like I said, the best-laid plans . . .)

No Way Off That Horse

But to look like a total idiot
and fall butt-first in the dirt,
so that's exactly what I did.

> *I thought your problem was*
> *sitting a trot, not gettin' off*
> *the horse.* Ethan stood over me.

Aunt J *told* him? My face
bubbled heat. "Apparently,
I've got multiple problems."

> Ethan's grin broadened.
> He offered a hand, pulled
> me to my feet. *Don't we all?*

Poncho snorted and moved
to one side, and the saddle
slid completely under his belly.

> *Hard to sit a horse sideways,*
> *Pattyn, least that's what*
> *I've always believed.*

"Really? Well, I didn't have much
of a problem with the sideways
thing. Now, straight up and down . . ."

> He laughed out loud. *We'll*
> *have to work on that, okay?*
> *Ready to put the old boy away?*

We'll have to work on that? Why
did I so like the sound of that?
God, he was good-looking!

                         Ethan undid what was left of my
                         cinch knot, hoisted the saddle
                         up over one shoulder.

I led Poncho back to his pasture,
Ethan so close his scent—
sunbaked skin—engulfed me.

                         I'm glad you could spend the summer
                         with your aunt. She doesn't get
                         much company out here.

At least she hadn't told him
everything. "I'm glad I came."
Getting gladder by the minute.

Ethan Helped Me

Feed and water the livestock,
all the time making small talk.

He was working
at the feed store
to help pay for his
next semester at
UC Davis. He
was going to be
a veterinarian.

I told him I had no clue
what I wanted to be.

His mom had
recently died and
his dad lived,
single, on eighty
acres, just a couple
of miles from
where we stood.

I told him my dad should
have stayed single.

He had no brothers
or sisters and was,
in fact, lucky to
have made it into
this world. His

mom had had problems
carrying babies.

I told him my mom was
the goddess of fertility.

He'd had a girl at
Davis, but when he
brought her home
for a visit, she took
a good look around
and decided Caliente
was beneath her—
meaning he was too.

I told him not even Death
Valley was beneath my ex.

He wasn't Mormon.

I told him I wasn't sure
I was either.

If He Thought I Was Nuts

He didn't say so, or even give me a look
    that did. The more we talked, the more
        I liked him, and that didn't scare me a bit.
    Finally, it struck me that he must have
come over for some particular reason.

Turned out, Aunt J had invited him
    to dinner. As we wandered back toward
        the house, she came out onto the porch.
    You two about ready for supper? Hope so,
'cause supper's about ready for you.

We went inside, washed up, and by the time
    we got to the table, dinner had already arrived.
        Fried chicken, mashed potatoes, green beans
    canned personally by Aunt J, homemade
apple crisp. Oh yes, and a bottle of good Merlot.

Not that I knew good wine from bad, and of course,
    the guilt train got rolling as soon as the cork popped.
        But somehow I managed to hop off that locomotive.
    Stan was the wine collector, said Aunt J. *I don't tap*
into the cellar often. Just for special company.

Delicious food, mellow wine, and Ethan's very
warm leg, real close to mine. From time to time,
our thighs touched and neither of us hurried
to pull them apart. Did he realize what he was
doing to me? Was I doing the same to him?

Half of Me Said Yes

I hadn't imagined it.
      He had kept his leg there.
I hadn't started it.
      He had initiated contact.
I hadn't insisted.
      He had enjoyed it.

The other half insisted
      I was crazy.
          He was perfect.
      I was plain.
          He was worthy of a rock star.
      I deserved a zero.
          He was all a man should be.
      I wasn't yet a woman.

I mean, physically I was,
yes. Mother Nature came
to call regularly.
But emotionally?
      I was about six years old,
      still Daddy's little girl,
      even though Daddy

couldn't care less
about me. How could
I expect any man
ever would?

Journal Entry, June 16

What is the matter with me?
Three months ago, I barely
knew boys existed.

First I couldn't get Justin
out of my mind, even though
I had no chance at him, ever.

Then it was Derek I thought I had
to be with, even though he was
a total jerk. (Should have known.)

Now it's Ethan—too old for me,
too good-looking for me, too
everything, except LDS.

So why this amazing attraction?
Why do I even think he might
be a little bit interested in me?

Even if he is interested, do
I want a summer fling? That
was great, see ya later?

And what if we actually fell in love?
How could it ever work out?
Just think if Dad found out!

Why can't I just forget about
guys? Do I want to end up like
Aunt J? Or worse, like Mom?

I Tend to Overanalyze

So the next day I tried not to think about him at all.
Let things happen as they're meant to, I told myself.

Aunt J was planting the garden, turning long, even rows
of dirt so rich you could breathe in the compost smell.

I helped her rake the soil smooth, enjoying the sun's
gentle pulse on my back and the mindless labor.

For an hour or more we worked quietly. Not a single
question popped into my head. Work is good for that.

But when we stopped for lunch and lemonade, *bam,*
bam, bam, there came the questions in rapid succession.

"How long were you and Uncle Stan married?" "How
did he die?" "Why didn't you ever have children?"

Lord, girl, you do ask personal questions, don't you?
Ah well, a week after our thirteenth anniversary,

Stan found out he had stomach cancer. He fought
it for almost a year, but it finally got the best of him.

I wanted children and we tried to have them, but I couldn't carry a baby to full term. After five miscarriages, I said enough.

That made me think of something Ethan said. "Ethan's mom had trouble carrying babies too. Isn't that weird?"

No, Pattyn, it's not. Now I'm going to tell you a little story, and it isn't very pretty. But it's honest-to-God true.

Another Ugly Story

I sat, fascinated,
as Aunt J remembered:

> *In the 1950s the U.S. government*
> *detonated nuclear weapons aboveground,*
> *down at the test site near Vegas.*

> *They didn't have a clear idea*
> *what radiation might do, so they*
> *tracked where the wind blew it,*
> *and what happened to those who*
> *came in contact with the fallout.*

I saw anger flash in her
steel gray eyes.

> *Your father and I were kids then,*
> *living near Ely. These men in suits,*
> *driving official-looking cars, would*
> *come around with these little badges*
> *to wear on the days they set off their bombs.*

> *They asked our family—and others—*
> *to sit outside and watch the blasts,*
> *which were visible hundreds of miles away.*

We learned a little
about them in school.

> The mushroom clouds were spectacular.
> Some people even had "blast parties,"
> drinking and carrying on as those venomous
> puffs lifted into the air and spread across the sky.

> The wind carried them, and those of us in its path
> became known as "downwinders." The closer
> you were to the test site, the more immediate
> the results—dead cattle, contaminated milk.

I remembered photos
of soldiers at ground zero.

> Afterward, the government men collected
> the badges, which turned black by degrees—
> the more radiation, the blacker they became.

> We were guinea pigs, Pattyn. Government
> guinea pigs. As the years wore on, the effects
> showed up in elevated cancer levels. And
> thousands of women suffered
> miscarriage after miscarriage.

That was something they
sure didn't teach in school.

> *It wasn't just in Nevada, either. That radiation
> went high into the atmosphere, moving across
> the country at will. There are downwinders in
> neighboring states, and even farther east.*

> *Today the government pays those of us still
> alive $50,000, if we can prove we were affected.
> I was one of the lucky ones. I survived breast
> cancer. Ethan's mother was not so fortunate.
> Neither was Stan, nor your Grandma Jane.*

"What about Dad and Grandpa
Paul? They're healthy."

> *Maybe their immune systems are stronger.
> Maybe their cancers are sleeping somewhere.
> Some people did stay healthy. Who knows why?
> They're probably part of some government study:
> "How Not to Die from Radiation Poisoning."*

> *Now the rest of the country wants Nevada to take
> its nuclear waste? Nevada is not a wasteland. We
> don't even use nuclear power. And Yucca Mountain
> sits right on top of an earthquake fault line.
> So much for the government's "sound science"!*

I hadn't really thought
about all that before.

> *I wish people could know my Nevada, see*
> *the beauty here. Mountains, reaching up into*
> *that cloudless blue sky. Rivers. Lakes. Forests.*
> *I wish they would consider our children, whose*
> *schools and parks sit beside the roads and tracks*
> *that will carry that irradiated crap.*
>
> *I wish they would think of someone*
> *besides themselves. You don't have a genie*
> *on you somewhere, do you? I'll climb down*
> *off my soapbox now. I've got beans to plant.*

Aunt J was right. Some of her
truths were not very pretty.

I Didn't Even Know

She'd had cancer.
Didn't know about her miscarriages,
or that she'd lost her husband
and mother to the creep of malignancies.

Learning all that made me
feel selfish for ever having pity
for myself. Compared to Aunt J's,
my life was a piece of cake.

I watched her in the garden,
tough as a backcountry winter,
despite pain no person should
have to bear, and I wondered

if she ever broke down
and screamed, ever thought about
hurting someone like she'd
been hurt (Dad, for instance).

Other questions smoldered
inside, burning their way
out of my brain, aiming
for my big mouth.

I figured I'd wait a day or two
to ask them, though. Aunt J
had opened herself wide.
I didn't want her to bleed out.

One Question Wouldn't Go Away

So as we worked together
on dinner, I posed it.
"Why did Dad want to go to
Vietnam? I mean, why fight
for a country that treated his own
family in such a terrible way?"

> Aunt J kept chopping broccoli.
> *We didn't know then. For years*
> *we had no idea that those beautiful*
> *mushroom clouds were angels*
> *of death. It took decades for someone*
> *to make the connection and start*
> *asking tough questions.*

"But why did it take so long?
I mean, dead cattle and poisoned
milk had to be a pretty big clue.
And what about incinerating
Hiroshima and Nagasaki? Couldn't
people put two and two together?"

America was innocent . . . and ignorant.
We believed this land was the chosen
land, and it was our duty to defend
it. The Japanese were the aggressors,
so they deserved their fate. But again,
we didn't know about the peripheral
deaths through radiation poisoning.

"Well then, what about government
agents, running around with
radiation badges? Didn't that raise
any alarms at all?" I could picture
the dark sedans, with G-men
in buzz cuts and perfect gray suits.

It was a different era, Pattyn. We
believed the people we voted into
power truly represented our interests.
Some still believe that, despite all
evidence to the contrary. But for
many, Vietnam opened the door
to questioning the status quo.

Newsreel segments came to
mind—American students
protesting the draft. Policemen
arresting them. Soldiers cutting
them down. "If Dad would have
known, would he have gone?"

> *I can't speak for Stephen, Pattyn.*
> *But my heart tells me yes. I don't*
> *think his joining the service had*
> *anything to do with ideals or moral*
> *obligation or even knowing that if he didn't*
> *join, he'd very likely get drafted.*
> *Soldiering was in his blood. . . .*

Her unfinished thought
drifted across the kitchen,
a heavy stink, tainting
the sweet summer air:

> Killing was in his blood.

Sleep Came Hard

That night. And
it wasn't just the moon,
shining full and bronze through
my bedroom window. Ever since I'd
been with Aunt J, I'd learned things—some,
like driving, were incredible things that I'd thought
I might never learn. Others were things I maybe didn't
want to know—that made me question every little corner
of my world, even the nooks I'd always felt safe tucked into.
Things like the truth about the law, so easily warped to fit the
circumstances; like government, not necessarily representative
of those who had created it—the people it was meant to serve;
like patriotism; the necessity of war, the wisdom of weapons
of mass destruction. Even things like school, preparing and
sacrificing for the future, with zero guarantee of a future
and no clue what kind it would be, should we happen
to find ourselves there. I stared wearily out at the
moon, shimmering, clean, in the pacific night
sky, and wondered if man had, indeed, set
foot on its mottled surface. And,
if we had, exactly what we
had left behind.

The Next Morning Before Dawn

I woke to crunching gravel as Ethan's
pickup pulled into the driveway,
horse trailer in tow.

Ethan. I smiled myself awake.

You gonna sleep all day? called Aunt J,
the screen door slamming
behind her.

I wrestled myself out of bed,

slipped into the Levi's she had loaned
me. They fit just like a pair
of jeans should.

Snug but not too tight.

Brushed my teeth. French braided
my hair. Wished I had
some makeup.

And knew how to use it.

But I didn't. What Ethan saw,
Ethan would get. Wait,
that wasn't right.

Or maybe it was exactly right.

We Saddled Up

Just past daybreak, the sun
glowing tangerine behind
a soft wash of morning.

Ethan's big black, Diego,
pawed impatiently as his human
tightened my cinch.

"No sideways riding, now,"
Ethan said, smiling. "That's just
plain showing off."

Old Poncho stood, still as a post,
as I tried to find a half-comfy
position for my bruised behind.

We started off at a gentle pace,
Aunt J on Paprika. The mare fit
her name—copper red, with a temper.

She's edgy today, said Aunt J.
*Been too long since she's waded
into a herd of longhorns.*

Edgy. Exactly. A jackrabbit
dashed across the trail and Paprika
danced into the air.

Better let her run. You up for speed?
Aunt J didn't wait for an answer.
Neither did Paprika.

Ethan's black was game. He
took off after the copper mare
like it was the Kentucky Derby.

Poncho responded with a butt-
jarring, teeth-rattling trot.
Plop-plop-plop-plop.

Aunt J looked back, laughed,
and yelled, *Let loose of the reins
and give him a kick.*

I did. Reluctantly, Poncho
launched into an easy canter.
Karoomp-karoomp-karoomp.

Diego caught Paprika
and the two ran neck and neck.
It was thrilling to watch.

Bouncing, sliding, and somehow
hanging on, Poncho and I followed
their dust for a quarter mile or so.

Finally, they slowed. *There they are,*
shouted Aunt J. *Just waiting for
someone to bring 'em to fodder.*

A longhorn is an awesome sight,
2000 pounds of beef, with horns
that could make the devil tuck tail.

Ninety cows and a bull, plus
calves in various sizes, dotted
a meadow just beyond a cattle chute.

*This drought has spent the low
meadow. We'll move 'em up-country,
on government land, for the summer.*

Howie! Maizie! Australian shepherds were born to herd. The dogs leaped into action and the cattle took notice.

Personally, I Took Notice of Ethan

I was never big on cowboy flicks, but watching
Ethan command that big horse was by far
the sexiest thing I had ever seen.
He didn't need the reins, but
moved the black by
shifting weight.

Their rapport—
musical, syncopated—
was a thing of incredible
beauty. I knew I wouldn't walk
right for days, but I didn't care. Just
being there was worth every bump and lump.

Through a stretch of barbed wire fence,
we entered public land, where cattle
could graze for a small fee
and, according to Aunt J,
a ration of shit from
the "greenies."

Not that I don't
think our environment
needs protection. But the
Good Lord blessed this country
with all the necessities for running beef.
I've got to believe that's what He had in mind.

We spent the better part of the day coaxing
the dogs, chasing strays, and otherwise
moving the herd up-mountain. It
probably seems dumb,
but I'd never had
so much fun.

The shadows
had stretched long toward
the east by the time we reached
the high meadow reservoir. Dogs, horses,
and longhorns took a good deep swallow, and just
about then I realized we'd be riding home in the dark.

But Aunt J Had Other Plans

With the cattle free to graze at will,
we unsaddled the horses, tied them on long
leads, and left them to the tall grass.
A perfume of green followed their munching.

I hadn't even noticed the bedrolls
and saddlebags. Once I did it became clear
we were spending the night.
I'd never in my life camped out under open sky.

Ethan and I gathered firewood as Aunt J
cleared a spot in the sand near the water. *The grass
is green, but we can't take a chance on settin'
a wildfire. Sand is tough to burn.*

A sudden urge hit and it came to me
I hadn't gone pee all day. How could I go now,
with Ethan right there? I pulled
Aunt J off to one side. "I really gotta go . . . you know."

She chuckled. *Ethan Carter, you turn
your head toward the lake, now. Don't move until
I say so.* Then she pointed toward
a nearby deadfall. *Your throne awaits you, Princess.*

I didn't feel much like royalty, squatting
behind that old dead tree, but I don't think Ethan
peeked. I'm pretty sure Derek would
have tried. He and his crew were definitely that type.

Anyway, as dusk rolled out its deep blue
carpet and the stars lit up, one by one, we sat around
the campfire, eating sandwiches and apples.
In the fringe of woods, coyotes fired up a serenade.

Hardly aware I was doing it, I scooted
a little closer to Ethan. He put a good-natured arm
around my shoulder. *You aren't afraid
of those varmints, are you? They won't bother us.*

His touch was electric. I didn't dare
move, didn't want to disturb the stunning connection.
My voice was barely a whisper. "It's just
a little spooky, being out here, so close to them."

I prayed he wouldn't take his arm away,
wouldn't leave me shaking in the descending darkness.
He didn't. Instead he pulled me in to him.
Don't worry, pretty lady. I'll keep you safe.

It was a moment to read about in a romance
novel, to see on a movie screen. All that was missing
was for him to turn his face toward
mine, tilt my chin, and part his sultry lips . . .

But even without the kiss,
it was magical.

We
Stoked
the Campfire

For the night, unfolded
the bedrolls. They were thin,
but the night was warm. Before very
long, Aunt J was sawing logs. Ethan and I lay, feet to the fire,
staring up at black Nevada sky, where I swear a billion stars
had shown their lovely faces. I'd never seen
such beauty in my life. "Do you
suppose anything lives
out there?" I asked.

Well,
of course,
Ethan answered.
The universe is a very big place.
Besides, I'd be real surprised if the Good
Lord didn't hedge His bets somehow. I think He
must be real disappointed in His humankind experiment.
I thought about that for a little bit, then asked,
"So you believe God really exists?
I used to think so, but lately
I'm not so sure I believe
in anything."

Not God.
Not family.
Surely not
love.

Ethan Propped Himself

On one elbow, looked
straight down into my eyes.

> *Can't
> you see Him, sleeping
> there in your Aunt Jeanette?*

> *Can't
> you hear Him, sighing
> through the junipers?*

> *Can't
> you smell Him, raining
> life down on the desert?*

He hesitated, unsure,
found what he needed
in my eyes, then finished,

> *Can
> you feel Him
> when I do this?*

Ethan reached down,
kissed me, long and deep
and sweet as a mountain spring.

And in that kiss was little
doubt of anything.
Especially love.

It Was the Kiss You Dream About

The one that makes you understand
what all the hype is about.

Nothing I'd done with Derek
had produced the kind of electricity
now sizzling through my arteries.

In fact, all I'd done with Derek—
the best of it, and the worst of it—
became instantly inconsequential.
(In fact, who was Derek?)

I didn't want Ethan to stop, and he
didn't for a very long time.

When he finally pulled away,

he stroked my cheek, brushed
my hair from my eyes, and said,
I hope that was okay.

"No," I whispered, hoarse
with want. "It wasn't okay at all.
It was pretty much perfect."

Good, he said, nesting down into
the tall grass. *Because, far
as I'm concerned,*

that's only the beginning.

But He Didn't Try to Escalate

Didn't even kiss me again. Instead,
he pulled me into his arms. My
ear settled against his chest as

he fell into a satisfied slumber.

It was all so natural, yet so completely
new, listening to the rhythm of his
breathing beneath my ear.

Only the beginning . . .

What that might mean was way too
frightening to consider. In my
limited realm of experience,

beginnings led to endings.

I ran my hand lightly over his body,
memorized muscle and bone.
He responded with a sigh.

I breathed him in.

He smelled of apples, horse, and well-earned sweat, which I somehow found attractive. He smelled real.

He was real. Wasn't he?

If I awoke in the morning to find him gone, would I think it was all a dream? Or would I more likely believe

it was all a mistake?

I Awoke

To the colorless pall of early morning,
and a hint of dew on my bedroll.

It took a few seconds to realize where
I was and when I did, the night before

absolutely seemed like only a dream.
And yet, there was Ethan, beside me.

> He rolled toward me, cracked one eye,
> and said, *Morning, m'lady. Sleep well?*

I smiled. "I'm not exactly sure. Last night
seems a bit hazy." (Where did I dig up "coy"?)

> Ethan pretended hurt. *Is that so?*
> *Well, tell me, how much is clear?*

"Let me see. I remember sitting by the fire,
ravenously consuming a cold supper . . ."

> *Okay, sounds like we were both in*
> *the same general vicinity. What else?*

"Something regarding coyotes . . .
and was there a discussion about God?"

> *God and extraterrestrial life. A deep
> philosophical dialogue. After that?*

"Hmm . . . I'm trying to remember, really
I am. Can you give me a little hint?"

> *With pleasure.* Our second kiss, though shorter,
> was every bit as memorable as the first.

Shorter Because Aunt J

Was already up and singing
a Garth Brooks ballad,
accompanied by the paw
of horses, an occasional
moo, and the good-
natured yip-yip of dogs.

She glanced our way, no
shock, no anger, then gave
a wink absent of "I told you so."
Sorry to say breakfast is more
of dinner, only staler. But I'm
betting you two are hungry.

Hungry, why? Exactly
how much did she know?
Surely she hadn't witnessed
the vivid scene the night
before! Had she seen us
sleeping head to shoulder?

Ethan excused himself
and wandered over behind
the deadfall. Aunt J took
the opportunity to observe,
Hope you got a little sleep.
It's a decent ride home.

I scooted out of my
bedroll, drew closer to
the morning campfire. So
much I wanted to say, but
where to start? I settled
for, "Thanks, Aunt J."

Her eyes, honest,
took hold of my own.
*Nothing to thank me
for. Just keep on shining
that light. The rest will
take care of itself.*

Without Cattle to Keep Track Of

The ride home
was more

         relaxed.

Even Old Poncho
seemed more

         at ease,

swaying his head
as he clomped along.

         Ethan

kept his black close
by my side,

         and I,

for the first time
in my life,

         felt

like anything was
possible, everything

         right.

For five hours,
in fact, I

         felt

so fine I didn't once
overanalyze the

         perfect

emotion, budding
inside. The

one

I'd always feared
most.

Closing In on Home

Aunt J reined in Paprika.
> *Ethan, Pattyn has never really had a taste*
> *of a good horse underneath her. Put her*
> *on back and give her a dose, would you?*

I climbed up behind him,
> shaking slightly, both at the idea of what
> was to come, and the idea of cinching
> my arms tight around him.

The black didn't much
> care for the notion of double, but Ethan
> was most definitely in control. The horse
> tensed as Ethan said, *Fasten your seat belt.*

I did as instructed, wrapping myself
> around him like duct tape. Aunt J took
> charge of Poncho as Ethan urged Diego
> forward. Two steps and we hit a dead gallop.

God, what a feeling! Beneath
> a layer of denim, the gelding's muscles
> flexed and pulsed as we picked up speed.
> I buried my face in Ethan's shirt, closed my eyes.

I was flying, no less than an eagle.

> I was belly to back with the most incredible
> man in the world, a man who had kissed me
> like I never expected to be kissed. Ever.

I was the luckiest girl in the world.

> Deep in my brain, I heard Aunt J's words.
> *True love finds you once, if you're lucky.*
> Had true love come knocking at my door?

Back at the Ranch

Ethan clearly didn't want to
leave right away, and Aunt J,
             bless her heart, said,
                 I appreciate your help. Least I can
                 do is offer you a hot supper.
                     Shouldn't take long.
Ethan and I walked the horses,
cooling them down before letting
             them eat or drink.
                 We paced in a large circle,
                 side by side, letting our bodies
                     touch, loving the touch.
Ethan was warmth in the cooling
night, a lantern in drawing darkness.
             Yet my high began to sink.
                 The events of the last two days had
                 left me breathless. I wanted more.
               Did I expect too much?
Ethan had something on his mind.
I could almost hear the churn
          of words inside his head.
                 My heart lifted into my throat.
                 Everything felt so right. Would he
                 tell me instead it was wrong?

As If Reading My Mind

Ethan stopped, took my hand.
Pattyn, hold on a second.
I'm not really sure what came over me . . .
No! Please no? Oh God, not
"had to happen sometime."
My face must have crumbled.
No, no. I'm not saying I made
a mistake. It just happened so fast.
Falling for you, I mean.
Falling? In love? In lust? Where
else could you fall? Without answers,
I didn't know what to say.
The first time I saw you—at the grocery
store that day—there was something
about you. Something sad, deep down sad . . .
How could I forget that day?
The day my father abandoned me.
The day I would forever thank him for.
But there was also a touch of redemption.
I wondered how the two could coexist
in the same soul. I was so sad myself. . . .
How could he have seen all that
in just one passing glance? On that
day I didn't feel very redeemed.

> *I wanted to know you. When I saw you*
> *with your Aunt Jeanette, I knew*
> *I'd get my chance.*

Ethan pulled me into his arms, kissed
my forehead. I looked up into
his eyes and found my answers.

> *I just want you to feel the same*
> *way. If you want me to back off,*
> *slow things down, I will.*

I shook my head. "Don't back
off, Ethan." I reached up, put
my arms around his neck,

and this time *I* kissed *him.*

Journal Entry, June 19

I can't sleep. Maybe I'll
never sleep again. Does your
brain ever shut down, once
you fall in love?

Am I in love?

It sure feels like love.
Ethan is everything any girl
could ask for. And he promises
he wants me. Why me?

Shut up, Pattyn. Quit asking
that question. Why even
care why he wants you?
Isn't it enough that he does?

I know guys lie.
Enjoy the game.

But I have to believe
Ethan is different.
Do his eyes lie?
His kisses?

When he kisses me, it's
like being born again.
Born where love isn't
just a word, but something
alive, throbbing with life.
That's how I feel tonight.
Throbbing with life.

Did Mom and Dad ever
feel like this?
For each other?
I want to believe it.

But I can't.

Ethan Started Stopping By

Every evening on his way home.
June was a hazy blur of days with Aunt J,
mostly spent in nervous anticipation
of evenings with Ethan.

Aunt J never said a disapproving
word, but after a week or so, she
did offer an obligatory warning.

You two seem to be getting
serious. I can't expect you
to keep saying no. But I hope
you know how to be careful.

Up till then, I hadn't had to say no.
Ethan treated me with nothing but
respect. But things had definitely heated up.

A time or two, cradled in his lap,
kissing until his desire became
obvious, I had almost wanted to.
But even though most of me

was a new, liberated Pattyn, traces
of the old, conservative Pattyn
lingered, hard to shake off.

The next-to-the-last thing I wanted
was a baby. The very last thing
I wanted was ever having to tell
my dad I was pregnant.

Thursday, June 29

Kicked off the extra-long
Fourth of July weekend.
      It also happened to be
      my seventeenth birthday.
            I truly expected a card
            from Mom and Dad.
                  Never arrived.
                  Never even got a call.

To be fair, Jackie sent
a card a few days late.
      Said girls' camp was
      entertaining, especially
            when they tried to freak
            everyone out with scary
                  stories about Satan
                  dropping in overnight.

She said Mom was about
as big as a dairy cow,
      'Lyssa had her first period,
      Teddie had her first crush,
            Davie got straight A's,
            Roberta lost her two front teeth,
                  Georgia still sucked her thumb,
                  and Dad was meaner than ever.

Everything pissed him off.
The window he had to pay
       for, the ER bill he had
       to pay for, tithing 10 percent
           when everything was up
            10 percent and he had a new baby
                coming. Diapers were up 10 percent.
                And Johnnie was up 20 percent.
I wanted to write her back,
tell her none of that mattered,
       that out here in the real world
       were people like Aunt J. And
           Ethan. I wanted to tell
           her everything about him.
                But I knew any letter from me
                would never get past my dad.

Back to My Birthday

What a celebration Aunt J planned!
We would drive into Cedar City, Utah,
(the nearest "big city") for a shopping
spree. Later, Ethan would join us
for dinner and a movie. A movie!

Wal-Mart served as Cedar City's
unofficial "mall." And that was close
enough for me. Stuff. Tons
and tons of stuff. Just looking at
all that stuff made me kind of delirious.

Sure, I'd been to Wal-Mart before, but
never after weeks of feed stores
and mini-marts. Aunt J planned
on stocking the pantry, and I planned
on having a great time helping her.

We strolled along the clothing aisle,
commenting on summer fashions.
Aunt J insisted I model blouses
and shorts and jeans. Anything I
liked went into the shopping cart.

I couldn't believe it. Store-bought
clothes were like gold in my house.
Owning Wally's was as good
as owning Old Navy or even Macy's.
And, hey, they carried Wranglers.

But there was more. Books. Music—
a small CD player and discs to go
in it. Pricey shampoo and sweet-
smelling lotion. Makeup. I tried
to protest, but Aunt J wouldn't listen.

It makes me happy to see a smile
on your face. Besides, I've got money
growing mold in the bank. Might
as well spend a little before I die.

We Spent More Than a Little

I won't confess exactly how much,
but I'd never before seen a register
ring up a total like that.

(Not even a week's worth
shopping trip for a family of nine!)

On the way to dinner, I slithered into
a new pair of jeans—my very first.
Is there anything quite as wonderful

as developing a relationship
with brand-new jeans?

Above them went a crocheted shell,
soft turquoise in color. Even I had to admit
it looked great over the tan of my arms.

(Not to mention muscles, newly
defined by yard work.)

Above that went a light brush of coral blush
(Aunt J said the color went best with my skin tone)
and a stroke or two of soft black mascara.

Somehow I managed it with
only the tiniest smear.

And when I stepped down from the pickup,
I felt a year older. A decade wiser.
Prettier than I'd ever believed I could feel.

That's how Ethan saw me when
he found us at the restaurant.

They Say the World Sees You

As you see yourself,
and that night I saw myself in a different way.

Pretty. Almost desirable.
Ethan's eyes told me I was both. And more.

He kissed me. In front
of the whole restaurant. *Happy birthday, Pattyn.*

We had so much fun
at dinner—authentic Mexican cuisine, the real deal.

Before that night, Taco Bell
had defined my total experience with Mexican food.

I let Aunt J order for me.
"Anything but tacos, please. I want to try something new."

Steak fajitas arrived
at the table, sizzling and steaming in a cast-iron skillet.

I polished them off and just
as I finished up, our waitress plopped a sombrero on my head.

Another waitress joined her,
carrying three plates of flan. One had a candle in the middle.

They sang "Feliz Cumpleaños,"
the Mexican equivalent of "Happy Birthday," and everyone clapped.

And as we left for the movie,
it crossed my mind that I didn't really need a birthday card from home.

Aunt J Surprised Me Again

*You two take in
the movie without
me. I'm tired and
it's a long drive
home for these
achin' bones.*

I tried to talk her out
of her plan, but Aunt J
could be stubborn.

*Only so much fun
an old woman
can take in one
day. Shoppin'.
Eating till I'm
ready to bust . . .*

I tried to thank her for
making my birthday more
special than any before.

*Pshaw. What are
birthdays for?
You'll take good
care of her, won't
you, Ethan? Not too
much candy, hear?*

Ethan laughed, kissed her
cheek, and promised
I was in very good hands.

Perfect Hands, Actually

They opened the Dakota's door, lifted me up
　　　　onto the seat. Ethan slid under the wheel,
sat for a moment, just looking at me.
　　　　Do you know how beautiful you are?

I shook my head. "I'm not. But you make
　　　　me feel like I am." I wanted to be beautiful.
To him. For him. I didn't really care how
　　　　anybody else saw me. Only Ethan.

He reached across me, opened the glove
　　　　compartment, extracted a little box wrapped
in gold foil. He cradled it in his perfect
　　　　hand, offered it to me like a toddler might.

Inside was an oval locket, etched
　　　　gold on a serpentine chain, and
inside that was a photo of Ethan.
　　　　So you'll always carry me with you.

I fingered the intricate carvings,
　　　　the interlocking links of chain.
And then I turned it over. Engraved
　　　　on the back were three magic words.

Ethan pulled me close, repeated
      those words. *I love you, Pattyn.*
He kissed me, delicious as honey.
      His kiss held love. His eyes held love.

Goose bumps erupted all over
      my body. I was thrilled. Terrified.
But I couldn't deny how I felt
      about him. "I love you, too, Ethan."

We Went to a Movie

Probably only the third in my life,
and my first ever with a guy.
I should remember everything
about it. But I don't.

I don't remember the names
of the actors, and all I can recall
about the plot is that everyone
thought the main character
was someone he wasn't.

(Aren't we all someone we're not?)

I do remember the smell of popcorn
as we walked through the door,
and whiny children, pleading
for candy and soda pop.

I remember how people seemed
to smile at us, a young couple,
hand in hand. I wondered
if they smiled because
they knew we were in love.
Or maybe they smiled
at what they imagined
we did in the dark.

Doing stuff in the dark
of the movie theater
is what I remember best.

I Also Remember the Drive Home

Tucked close beside Ethan,
his picture tucked   close
to my heart, where I would
carry him   always.

He drove slowly, and we
talked and talked about our   lives
BE (before each other),
and what might become
of our lives now that they   intertwined.

How would we keep our   love
alive, with him at college
and me at school,
daily existence   at odds.

Where would I go to school?
No one had mentioned
if or when my extended
vacation might end.
If I stayed   with
Aunt J, my school would
be seven hundred miles
from Ethan's.

If I went home, our schools
would be less than two
hundred miles apart.
Not an insurmountable
distance. Unless you
figured in   my dad.

Of course, there were
ways around my dad.
Weren't there?

Even If There Were

Ways around my dad,
did I want to have to find them?
                    Did I want to go home?
Living with Aunt J had opened
my eyes. To harsh realities.
                    Harsh realities smoldering at home.
To the true meanings of love.
Love, like between Aunt J and me.
                    Love I wouldn't find at home.
Love, like I had discovered
in Ethan's arms.
                    Love that home might destroy.
But if I stayed with Aunt J,
Ethan seven hundred miles away,
                    what would become of our love?

Three Magic Words

Had changed my existence
yet again, words I'd feared
and now embraced.

I love you played over
and over in my brain,
music without melody.

I sat very close, almost
in his lap, head against
his shoulder, breathing

him in, hand on his thigh.
He was warm, and my warmth.
Strong, and my strength.

Ethan was no summer
fling. Suddenly, certainly,
he was everything.

How could I
ever live without him?

We Agreed Not to Worry

About it the rest of the weekend,
five whole days to spend together,
culminating with the July Fourth
BBQ and fireworks extravaganza.
I would meet Ethan's dad that evening.

Meanwhile, I wanted one thing—
okay, I wanted several, but I had
one particular goal in mind,
which I brought up on Saturday.
"Ethan, will you teach me to ride?"
And not Old Poncho. "Paprika."

Ethan was patient. Not so Paprika.
She took one look at the total "greenhorn,"
and decided to teach me the finer
points of equine bitchery.

She snorted.   Kicked.   Rooted
herself and   refused   to move.

When I finally convinced her otherwise,

she lowered   her head   and bucked.
Then she   reared and   pawed the air.

319

I dropped the reins, grabbed hold of the horn,
and somehow stayed in the saddle.
But it wasn't what you'd call pretty.

Aunt J Had Come Out

To watch
my progress—or lack of it.

> *She doesn't like working behind*
> *fences. Take her out on the trail*
> *for a real ride.*

First, Aunt J gave
me some pointers.

> *The key to Paprika is letting her*
> *think she's getting her way.*
> *Don't fight her. Convince her.*

Ethan clarified, *Gentle*
hands, gentle legs.

> *Let the reins all the way loose,*
> continued Aunt J. *Now give*
> *her an easy nudge.*

Instinct insisted I tighten my
grip, but I did as instructed.

> *There now, see how sweet*
> *that mare moves? Just*
> *like a rocking horse.*

A rowdy rocking horse,
but she was cooperating.

> *Teamwork. With Paprika,*
> *it's all about teamwork.*
> *Ask her to lope.*

Lope? At my confused look,
Ethan said, *Canter.*

> *A little tap with your
> heels should do. Remember,
> it's a request.*

I requested. Paprika
responded enthusiastically.

> *Now shift your weight to one
> side, see how she moves
> right along with you.*

I shifted right. Paprika
moved right. Left, left.

> *That's it! Damn if you
> don't look like a real
> working cowgirl!*

After an hour of coaxing
and correcting, I almost felt
like one too.

The Idea of a Trail Ride

Half scared, half excited me.
But Ethan insisted I'd be fine,
         so he went home for his black.

We hit the trail early afternoon,
         jogging down the jeep track
well beyond the cattle chutes.

         Paprika was up for a gallop, and
so was Diego. Ethan and I gave
         the horses their heads. What a rush!

If you've never ridden a horse at a dead
         run, you can't understand the awesome
power beneath your clinging thighs.

         It was total fear and total exhilaration,
all wrapped up in one amazing bundle
         of horseflesh. And I (mostly) controlled it.

With much of her energy spent, Paprika
         went docilely along with the game plan.
Ethan and I rode for miles and miles.

We paralleled a snake of train tracks,
smack beneath steep ledges of granite,
        sandstone, and minerals I couldn't identify.

The cliffs were beautiful and dangerous.
        Boulders, some the size of VWs, had
tumbled down to land like solitary soldiers.

        Ethan pointed. *That's where they'll run their
nuclear waste shipments. Can you believe
        what total idiots they are? One rock slide . . .*

I considered a head-on between a nuke train
        and VW-size boulders. One rock slide
and everyone for miles around would be toast.

We Stopped for Lunch

On a shady bank
of the little stream
bisecting the canyon.
  "Thank you, Ethan."

    The horses munched
    contentedly as Ethan
    unrolled a bamboo mat.
      What for, pretty lady?

I let myself recline,
to better inspect
the cloudless July sky.
  "For teaching me to ride . . ."

    Ethan lay down beside
    me, took my hand and
    kissed my fingers.
      You're a quick learner.

I closed my eyes,
loving the wet of his
tongue on my fingertips.
  "For showing me this country . . ."

He lifted up on one
elbow, and his voice
drifted down over me.
    I want to show you the world.

Drowsy with heat
and the lull of his touch,
I licked my lips.
    "For loving me."

He tilted my chin
and I looked up into
his electric green eyes.
    Let me teach you what love is.

His Body Settled

Gently upon mine.
    He kissed my eyes,
        my lips, my neck,
            then his mouth
                crept softly down
                    the length of my torso.

Something stirred
    beneath my skin,
        some being inside
            I'd only suspected
                existed, demon or
                    angel, I couldn't say.

Either way, it woke
    a desire so bold
        it shook me to my
            core, made me cry
                out for more. I
                    wanted all of Ethan.

And he wanted me,
    I felt it in the fire
        of his kiss, in the way
            his body trembled.
                And yet, he hesitated.
                    Only if you're sure.

The old Pattyn had
      vanished, smoke.
            I didn't think about
                 Satan, didn't think
                     about God, didn't
                         think about babies.

We shed our shirts,
      unzipped our jeans,
            and would have
                 made love right
                     that minute except
                         for just about then . . .

All Hell Broke Loose

From a snag of rocks across
the stream, and not a hundred feet
away, came a predatory snarl.

The horses reacted with terrified
whinnies and vicious thrusts
of defensive hooves.

Ethan and I jumped to our feet,
caught sight of the feline intruder—
a cougar, the size of a Great Dane.

He had wandered down the hill
for a midday drink, to find horses
and half-naked humans.

Ethan or I was the easier meal,
especially once the horses tugged
loose and bolted for home.

The mountain lion approached
leisurely, intently, measuring
distance and possible resistance.

Ethan groped in the tall grass,
found a tree branch big enough
to do some damage.

Back away slowly, he instructed.
If he comes after me, you run,
you hear me? Run toward the road.

Then he pulled himself up very
tall and strode toward the lion,
screaming at the top of his lungs.

I could have run then, probably
should have run then. Instead, I picked
up a sizeable rock and screamed too.

At our noisy advance, the cougar
paused, glancing warily back
and forth between Ethan and me.

Every hunter gets a moment.
This was mine. I took dead
aim, heaved the rock.

It flew straight to its mark,
hit the cat in the rib cage
with a tremendous *thunk*.

The animal *yeowl*ed in protest,
and Ethan hefted the branch
like a batter waiting for a pitch.

But the cougar turned on his
haunches and retreated
up the hardscrabble hillside.

We waited a few minutes,
making sure he didn't
change his mind.

Finally, Ethan relaxed
his batter's stance, grinned.
Not bad, for a girl.

Then He Laughed

Evaluation.

And I did too, because his eyes
held admiration. Adoration.

*Has anyone ever told you how great
you look with your shirt off?*

Not bad,

I glanced down at my chest, covered
only by a thin sports bra and a sheen of sweat.

I thought, before a sudden wave of nausea
made me sink to my knees.

courageous?

My stomach churned around a knot of confusion.
Had my hunter's moment been insane or

incredible.

Ethan rushed to me, pulled me into his arms.
Don't worry. He's gone. And you were

*Still, we'd better find our clothes and head
for home. We've got a really long walk . . .*

enough

He didn't say it, but I thought it—the addendum
we both worried about. Had the cat had

for one day? Or would he follow along?

Either Way, We Had No Choice

But to put one foot in front
of the other, and hope we

   might come across the horses,
   grazing somewhere along the trail.

We plodded together in silence
for quite a while. Finally Ethan said,

   I wish I would've brought my gun.
   Normally I would have.

"I wish you would have
too. Why didn't you?"

   I thought it might upset you. Some gir—
   some people don't much care for guns.

"You should have asked, Ethan.
So happens I like guns fine."

   Really? He tugged me to a halt.
   You are full of surprises.

I smiled. "What's more,
I'm a pretty good shot."

He laughed. *I'll bet you are.
I'll just bet you are.*

We Started for Home Again

And once again fell quiet,
        both of us lost in thought
about the day's events.
        Around then it hit me
that I had been ready
        to give Ethan the most
personal part of me,
        and give it happily,
without a single worry
        about cause and effect.

                Ethan was troubled too.
                        Pattyn, you know I love
                you, and I want to make
                        love to you so much it
                hurts. But hurting you
                        is the last thing I want.
                Please don't say yes
                        just to make me happy.
                It has to be something
                        you want to happen too.

"Oh, Ethan, I do. I thought
        I'd be scared, but I'm not,
with you. The only thing
        that worries me is getting
pregnant. I could never
        have an abortion. And
I don't want to have a
        baby. Not now. And my
dad is crazy. Crazy
        enough to kill us both."

> We'll be careful, Pattyn.
>   I would never expect you
> to have an abortion. I do
>   want children someday,
> maybe even with you, but
>   now is not the time. And
> I would never put your life
>   in danger. Not from
> your father. And never again
>   from a mountain lion.

Never Say Never

But that story is yet to come.
We had probably walked
two hours when a cloud of dust,

heading our direction,
signaled probable rescue.
Aunt J braked the old Ford,
jerked her head out the window.

> *There you are, thank the Lord.*
> *I was hoping I wouldn't have*
> *to call in the troops. Search*
> *and Rescue hates these hills.*

Seems Aunt J had once taken
a tumble, not far away, on a
wooded bluff. Broke her leg
in several interlocking places.

> *Stan didn't even start to worry*
> *until it got dark. By then it was*
> *too late to start a search. I spent*
> *a cold, helpless night up there.*

Which led us to the reason
for our own dilemma. Ethan
told the story, minus the naked
part, about the cougar.

Don't like the sound of that.
Tomorrow I'd better go up
and check on the herd. I'm
afraid of what I might find.

*J*ournal Entry, July 1

What an incredible day.
So much happened, it's hard
to write it all down, so here
are the highlights, in
semichronological order:

* I rode Paprika, first in the paddock,
then on the trail.

* Ethan and I came really, really
close to making love.

* We would have made love,
except for the cougar.

* I splatted the cougar with
a rock, right in the side.

* The horses bolted, so Ethan and I
had to walk most of the way home.

* Aunt J is afraid the cougar
is killing calves.

* Tomorrow we'll ride up and
check on the herd.

* After dinner, Ethan and I talked.
Talked and kissed. Kissed
and touched. Touched.

Why is that so much
better now that he told
me he loves me?

He loves me.
And all I can think of,
lying here in bed,

despite all that happened
this incredible day,
is I wish

Ethan was lying next to me.

After Paprika

Poncho was a piece of cake,
a rather bland slice. I actually
felt envious, watching Aunt J
sashay along on Paprika.

> We hit the trail early and rode
> at a quick clip, anxious to locate
> the herd. Howie and Maizie scouted
> ahead and barked an alarm around noon.

The longhorns were scattered
across a grassy hillside.
Belying the otherwise peaceful
scene, buzzards circled overhead.

> Aunt J urged speed. Paprika
> and Diego responded. Poncho
> and I did our best, but as usual
> couldn't keep up.

When we finally caught them,
Aunt J and Ethan were kneeling
beside a tattered calf carcass.
Only the belly was missing.

The cat isn't killing for food, observed Aunt J. *He's killing for fun. And it won't stop until he's stopped.*

Ethan Agreed

Some cats get a thrill out of killing
just to hear an animal scream.

> *Some people are the same way,*
> *said Aunt J. Gotta stop them, too.*

You can't lock up a lion, Ethan
said. *It will take a bullet.*

> *I'm afraid you're right. Better round*
> *up a hunting party.*

Ethan said he'd draft a couple
of friends and come along.

> *The sooner the better. Early*
> *tomorrow, if possible.*

Think we should call Fish
and Game first? Ethan asked.

> *Too many questions will slow us down.*
> *Besides, the outcome will be the same.*

Part of his turf is private land,
Ethan said. *We can start there.*

Aunt J nodded. *No one needs to know where we finally bring him down.*

I wasn't about to get left behind.
"Can I go too? Please?"

I know you shoot for sport, but have you ever hunted an animal wilier than you?

I Had to Admit

That rabbits were about as

wily

as it got. But I wanted to

hunt

that cat with a desire so

bold

it surprised me. The new

Pattyn

was more than a coffee

addict,

more than a budding

sex fiend.

She was a blossoming

thrill seeker,

enchanted by each new

high

to happen her way.

Tracking

a mountain lion,

senses screaming,

no guarantee who

the victim,

or the prey, would

be? The new and improved

was definitely up for that.

ultimately

Pattyn

It Wasn't Hard

For Ethan to find a crew
eager for a cougar hunt.
He and two friends arrived
early the next morning.

Mike was tall and round,
Mark was wiry and short,
and they both carried custom
firearms, guaranteed deadly.

Ethan had a well-used 30.06.
Slide-bolt actions and large-
bore barrels only vaguely
familiar, I felt the odd man out.

Aunt J handed me a 30-30,
showed me how to load
the chamber, and warned,
Careful now, it's got a kick.

The gun wasn't as heavy
as I'd feared, and it had a great
little scope. I figured I could
deal with a bit of a recoil.

She only carries six bullets,
so you'll have to make your
shots count, said Aunt J.
You won't have time to reload.

Six bullets? No problem.
It would only take one.

We Took the 4x4s

Drove to the site of Ethan's and my
debauchery, set off on foot in the direction
of the mountain lion's hasty departure.

We crossed the stream, located his tracks
on the muddy bank. *That's a jim-dandy
cat*, observed Mark, squatting to take a better look.

With no proper trail, we scrambled up over
granite boulders, slipping on slides of shale.
The 30-30 thumped against my ribs.

The top of the hill was almost treeless,
only solitary evergreens to break
the gray monotony.

Mike nodded his slightly balding
head. *Lion country, all right. You
can see clear to Caliente.*

A slight exaggeration, but disquieting
nonetheless. Still, I felt no fear.
There was safety in our numbers.

*We're looking for scat, prints, maybe
his leftovers,* Ethan explained.
Spread out, but stay in each other's sight.

We all fell silent, knowing the cat
would tune in to unusual sounds.
Softly, we moved apart and forward.

It wasn't easy, searching for clues
across an expanse of desert stone.
I bent low as I walked, squinting for signs.

July sun pounded my back, raised
a sweat to sting my eyes. Finally,
I stood to mop it away.

Where had everyone gone?

I Didn't Want to Shout

I knew they couldn't be far.
　　　　I was still moving north,
assumed they must be too.

Glancing around, I discovered
　　　　the source of my dilemma—
I had wandered up a narrow channel.

It cut between monolithic slabs
　　　　of ancient granite, gray
and time-polished and tall.

It wasn't a dead end. I could
　　　　see clear through to the far
side, so I stayed on course.

I walked slowly, hugged
　　　　the shade of the giant rocks.
Still, I rained perspiration.

Suddenly, I sensed movement
　　　　above my head. I looked up,
saw nothing. Heard no sound.

A shiver of fear traveled
        the length of my spine, though
my eyes could find no reason.

I scooted back against one side.
        Opposite me, gravel trickled
down the face of the rock.

Something was up there,
        all right. Should I run?
Freeze? Scream for help?

Not twenty feet away, the cougar
        slunk into view, assessed
his prey, snarled a promise of battle.

I opened my mouth, but the shout
        stuck fast in my throat. A single
thought entered my brain. The rifle.

The cat snarled louder, maneuvered
        himself into a better position as
my right hand reached for the gun.

I willed myself not to panic,
       lifted the rifle, tried to sight,
but my shaking arms denied me.

Above and slightly in front of me,
       the lion, all tooth and sinew, tightened
his haunches for the pounce.

My finger squeezed, the rifle belched,
       the bullet ricocheted off the rock,
well below my would-be assassin.

He didn't even flinch as he leaped.
       I'm going to die, I thought, my eye
catching a glimpse of four-inch claws.

Suddenly, a loud *crack* shook
       the rock walls. Ethan's shot caught
the cat midair, dropped him at my feet.

I stared, horrified, as he moaned
       and twitched. I swear he stared
at me as he stuttered his last breath.

My arm ached from the rifle's recoil,
        my ears rang from the echoed report,
and my heart pounded in my brain.

I watched the cat's life ebb away,
        and didn't know whether to feel
relief, satisfaction, or remorse.

Ethan Sprinted Toward Me

I think he was yelling something,
but I'm not really sure.

Because right about then, the ground
reached out and grabbed me.

Then everyone came running,
yelling and asking questions:

What happened? You got him?
Are you all right?

Mark and Mike took charge
of the cat corpse.

Aunt J and Ethan took charge
of me, or wanted to.

They tried to help me to my feet,
but I shook them off,

insisted I could take care of myself.
Like I'd really proved *that*, hadn't I?

I'm Not Sure Why

I felt so angry, but on the ride
home, I didn't sit plastered to Ethan,
and I barely said one word.

> Finally, he asked,
> *Okay, what's wrong?*

I shook my head. "I just can't
believe how stupid I was. If
it wasn't for you . . ."

> He reached over and pulled
> me closer. *Everything's okay.*

"No, it's not. I mean, I'm
grateful to you for coming
to my rescue, but . . ."

> Ethan turned and looked
> me in the eye. *But what?*

"But what if you hadn't
been there? I should have
been able to take that shot."

> *It was a hard shot, Pattyn,*
> *even for someone with experience.*

It was a hard shot, yes.
But, "I wasn't paying attention.
The cat got the drop on me."

*One thing you have to remember
when hunting predators . . .*

"Yes?"

It pays to be a better predator.

Ethan Didn't Stay

For dinner that night,
sensing my need to be

alone.

I know it may sound
weird, but looking

death

square in the eye
made me question the

unknown.

What happens after
we exhale our last

breath?

Do we really see
an otherworldly

light?

Does God send
angels to guide us

home?

Or when our eyes
close, do we forfeit

sight?

And will our earthly
spirits forever

roam?

The Questions Ran Deeper

For me, struggling
with Mormon doctrine.
According to scriptures,
long pounded into my brain,
I was not worthy
of the Celestial Kingdom—
the highest level of Heaven.

I had not learned the secret
codes to open that door,
and I had no Mormon
husband to let me in.

And did I want the Celestial
Kingdom, anyway, where
women are relegated
to polygamy and procreation,
gestating new souls to fill
earthbound bodies?

Would I truly become a goddess—
albeit a baby factory goddess—
should I actually find my
way to the Celestial Kingdom?

Would my spirit be happier
wandering the Terrestrial
Kingdom—planet Earth—
forever?

Would the almost-sins I'd
already succumbed to condemn
me to the Telestial Kingdom,
the place where scumbags go?

Was Heaven something
different from all of the above?

Had that cougar killed me,
where would I be now?

I Lay on the Bed

My head a jumble
of questions that I knew
would find no answers
until I actually died.

Fear closed in. Fear
of the unknown.

Fear of what I'd
been taught to be
unshakable truth.

Fear of what I hoped
would prove to be
unspeakable lies.

My very foundation shook,
an earthquake in my gut.

I was all new, right?
So why did the old Pattyn
surface now?

I loved Ethan so intensely
I just might die without him.

But what if loving him
damned me to death,
no chance of life after?

Was loving him now
enough to turn my back
on eternity?

Journal Entry, July 2

I could have died today,
probably would have, except
Ethan shot the cougar who
had decided to make me lunch.
That made me wonder if there's
one Heaven or three kingdoms,
or anything at all after we die.
I have no idea what to believe.

I asked Aunt J what she believes.
She said she's come to think
there is a God, but He isn't like
the God I've been taught to fear.

"God is love," she said. "And He
respects love, whether it's between
a parent and child, a man and woman,
or friends. I don't think He cares
about religion one little bit. Live your
life right, Pattyn. Love with all your
heart. Don't hurt others, and help
those in need. That's all you need
to know. And don't worry about
Heaven. If it exists, you'll be welcome."

*I hope God respects how I feel
about Ethan. Because I love him
more than anything, even life itself.*

Having Decided That

I was all smiles when he came
over the next morning, pickup
packed and readied for the trip
to Beaver Dam State Park.

> *It's gonna be hot as blazes,*
> Ethan said. *Grab your swimsuit.*

Swimsuit? Good Mormon
girls kept their clothes on. Of
course, I wasn't exactly good,
and maybe I wasn't Mormon.

> Ethan must have read my mind.
> *I promise to be a gentleman.*

Fact was, I didn't even own
a swimsuit. No tanks,
definitely no bikinis. "I . . .
I forgot to bring mine."

> Ethan smiled. *No problem.*
> *We can go in our underwear.*

I wasn't sure about that,
wasn't sure I wanted to reveal
so much skin—chalk white,
except for the arms and legs.

> Ethan lifted me up into the truck.
> *Let's go. It's a long drive.*

Not so far, distance-wise,
only around thirty-five miles. But
most of that was gravel road,
and slow, bumpy traveling.

I'm glad you're feeling better
today. I was worried.

"I'm sorry, Ethan. I don't
know why I got so upset.
Half of me feels so together,
the other half so confused."

Confused about what,
Pattyn? Me?

"Not about loving you, Ethan.
Just about what that means."
Did it mean damnation?
Happily ever after?

Ethan Was Right

It was hot as blazes.
By the time we reached the lake,
around noon, the temperature
had soared well into the nineties.
The lake was blue and very small,
too small for boats, so it wasn't
nearly as crowded as I'd expected.

We found a secluded place to park,
hiked up under a thick stand of trees,
and spread a thick blanket
on a pine-needle carpet.
Ethan opened an ice chest
filled with soda and beer.
I could have chosen Coke.
I didn't.

Beer had never been my favorite,
but it tasted fine, ice-cold,
on such a torrid day.
Only one problem—I had
skipped breakfast. Before I knew
it, my head felt full of bubbles
and my tongue five inches thick.

Not that Ethan hadn't brought
food. He had—huge deli sandwiches,
carbs and protein to fend off
any impending hangovers.
But that day, that hour, that moment,
a blossoming buzz felt too great
to fight with food.

So When Ethan Suggested Swimming

I didn't hesitate to sprint down to the water's
edge. The sun attacked and my head spun
and the sand threatened to blister my
feet and it all encouraged me to
shed every stitch and dive
into the cold, clear water.
I didn't think to do a toe
test and surfaced, sputtering.
Ethan laughed and caught me in
goose-bump-covered arms, hugging
me close. All hints of self-consciousness
dissolved, and my nakedness felt delicious

wrapped in Ethan's water-chilled skin. *I love
you,* he said, *and I don't know what that
means either, only that you're the most
important thing in my life. And I
don't want to be without you.*
Then he kissed me with
a passion he'd not before
revealed. I tasted heaven. No
doubt of this heaven, no worries
about which kingdom I'd attained,
only the certainty that heaven, indeed,
existed, right there in our perfect union.

No, We Didn't Make Love

Right there in the water,
but we did merge
in a powerful way.

That connection, skin
to skin, no barriers, touched
brain as much as body.

It was more than a physical
awakening, more than
the pulse of human closeness.

Ethan felt like part of me,
something that couldn't
be excised without bleeding.

Our love was beginning
to feel like "forever" love,
a love to carry to the grave.

And, buzzed as I was,
I knew in my heart
it wasn't just the beer talking.

People Walked By

And I could sense their eyes,
trying to pry beneath the water.

> I didn't care one bit if they managed
> to see some forbidden something.

When they were out of sight,
Ethan and I dashed for our clothes.

> He put on his boxers, I put on my long
> T-shirt, nothing more except sandals.

Cool and wet, we wandered back
to our blanket, hand in hand.

> We both had another beer, thinking
> we should postpone the inevitable.

Finally, I flopped down on my back,
inviting his kiss . . . and more.

> *If I kiss you, I won't want to stop,*
> *don't know if I could.*

"I know, Ethan," I whispered, scared
and excited and uncertain and not unsure at all.

> And so he kissed me, everywhere,
> making me want to say yes even more.

And he wanted me, too, and he showed
me how to make him want me more.

> It all felt so right, so how it should
> be, that I begged him not to stop.

But he paused, long enough to find
the protection he'd brought along.

> While I waited, every nerve shouted
> out to be pacified. And when he did . . .

I Cried

It wasn't that it

       hurt

because, except
for a brief flash of

       pain

it all felt perfectly
wonderful, perfectly

       right.

Our bodies meshed,
one, incredibly

       in sync.

In Ethan's arms,
I knew no

       fear,

in this ultimate act
of giving, no

       foreboding.

I cried for what
I had

       lost,

my best-kept
secret,

       given away.

I cried for what
I had

                              gained,
the knowledge
of Eden, irrevocably

                              learned.

In the Aftermath

I lay shivering, bathed
    in oppressive heat.
Ethan's promises soothed,
    every syllable sweet.

He held me tightly,
    as if he thought I'd flee.
But I could never run
    fast enough to break free

of the demon I'd unleashed.

I loved Ethan just as much as
    I had a few minutes before.
In the light of what we'd shared,
    perhaps I loved him more.

But when I closed my eyes
    I didn't see Ethan's face.
Another silhouette appeared
    in that dark and dappled space.

It resembled my father.

A Couple More Beers

Made Daddy's face disappear,
but mostly because the rest of the day
is pretty much a blur.

We took another icy dip,
washing away evidence.
Still, I didn't feel exactly clean.

Ethan insisted I try some lunch,
great deli sandwiches
that tasted like cardboard.

Then we settled down beneath
low, lacy branches for a nap
before driving home.

I woke, minus the buzz, plus
a pounding headache. In fact, I ached
in places I never knew could ache.

Yet there was Ethan, beside me,
looking more incredibly beautiful than ever.
He whispered a drowsy *I love you*.

And I settled into his arms, minus
the buzz, plus a pounding headache, and I
said, "Make love to me."

Journal Entry, July 3

Okay, we did it. Ethan and I
made love. Twice. The first
time it kind of hurt, and maybe
I had too much beer to really
understand what a big step
it was. Huge.

Nothing can ever again be
exactly the same.

The second time it was better,
even if I didn't feel so hot.
(My first hangover—ugh!)
Ethan is so gentle, so caring.
Derek would have attacked,
done the deed, and disappeared.
I'm so glad it was Ethan.

There were a couple of bad
moments—I'll be sore for days.

And tonight the guilt train
is rolling right across my brain.
When we came through the door,
Aunt J took one look and I swear

she knew the whole score.
That woman is psychic! Or maybe
our body language gave it away.

I'm not worried about Aunt J.
But Dad is a whole other story.

The Fourth of July

Dawned warm and bright.
I stayed late in bed, covers kicked
off, not asleep but thinking
about the day before.

Where did it leave Ethan
and me? Would we have to
make love every time we
saw each other?

Maybe I wanted that? I
did and I didn't. I mean,
I didn't want that to become
all we were about.

And yet part of me wanted
to fall right back into his arms,
to let him carry me up and away
over that sensual rainbow.

I was more confused than ever.
More in love than ever.
More worried than ever about
what would happen if

and/or when my parents found out.
Only a tiny fraction of me worried
about God. It was way too late
to stress over His judgment now.

Eventually

Aunt J called me downstairs.
    If she was, indeed, suspicious,
        she never said a word. Instead
            she asked, *How about helping*
                out with the pie baking?

There's something therapeutic
    about cutting shortening into
        flour, rolling the dough into
            thin rounds, then slicing
                apples and peaches,

adding sugar and cornstarch
    and pinches of spices until
        all those basic ingredients
            become perfect brown pies,
                cooling on the kitchen counter.

Aunt J and I worked for three
    hours, talking and laughing
        and fighting sweat in the
            gathering heat, half oven,
                half July, come to call.

Finally, she ventured, *Looks*
        like you and Ethan are getting
                serious. He's a fine young man,
                        Pattyn. Still, I am ultimately

responsible for how things
        turn out. I hope you know
                that I've come to love you
                        like my own daughter. I
                                don't want to see you hurt.

It Was a Stunning Admission

For a woman of few words,
a woman who let her eyes
say what her lips often wouldn't.

> Her admission deserved
> my own, "I love you, too,
> Aunt J. And I love Ethan."

>> *I know you do, little one.*
>> *And I believe he loves you.*
>> *If only love were enough . . .*

> "I wish I could promise
> I won't get hurt. I can't. But
> I have to take that chance."

She knew, too well,
the probable consequences
if it all came crashing down.

> "Aunt J, I've begged for love
> for seventeen years. Without you,
> I would never have found it."

God knows I would like to believe
otherwise. If ever a child
deserved love, it's you, Pattyn.

"Well then . . ." I smiled. "Looks
like we're on the same page.
Because you deserve love too."

We hugged, passing a jolt
of love between us, then
went back to our baking.

Once the Chicken Was Fried

And the salads made, Aunt J
and I went upstairs to change.

She spent a long time
in the bathroom, washing

and plaiting her long copper
hair and—I noticed when

she finally reappeared—applying
a ladylike amount of makeup.

She had chosen to wear a yellow
sundress, which showed off

her tanned, muscular arms
and hugged her bodice tightly.

In cutoffs and a pink tank top,
I was definitely outclassed,

and the way she smelled—
ginger and English lavender—

was enough to make any
cowboy swear off his herd.

Did she expect a special cowboy
at the evening's festivities?

Independence Day

Is a big deal in Caliente.
Hard-working people,
ready to let down and
party, make for a rowdy
crowd. The drinking
and socializing start
early, go all day.

Aunt J and I got to the
park at about three P.M.,
lugging a big canopy,
baskets, and coolers,
filled with enough
food for twenty.

Ethan and his father
were due to arrive
anytime. While
we waited, we sat
tapping our toes
to live—and very
loud—country music.

I Finally Spotted Ethan

Weaving through the crowd.
Beside him was a man who
could have been his brother, if not
for the salt-and-pepper hair.
Ethan's father was every bit as
handsome as he was.

Every now and then, they'd
stop to talk to people they knew
and a couple of times fingers
pointed in our direction.
Small town, everyone knows
everyone, and where they're sitting.

As they drew nearer, I noticed
Aunt J straighten her posture,
find her prettiest smile.
Ethan's dad was her special
cowboy? Why had she never
mentioned anything?

Finally, they found their way
over to us. Ethan pulled
me to my feet, gave me a big
kiss, then introduced us.

*Dad, this is Pattyn. You already
know her Aunt Jeanette.*

I couldn't have guessed
the drama that unfolded next.
But in retrospect, there had
been plenty of hints.
I'd just been so busy worrying
about myself that I never noticed.

Ethan's Dad Gave Me a Hug

So glad to finally meet you, Pattyn.
Ethan talks about you all the time.

Then he turned to Aunt J. *Hello,*
Jeanette. You look wonderful.

> Aunt J blushed like wine.
> *Good to see you again, Kevin.*

Kevin? Not her once forever
love, Kevin?

> *I'm so sorry about Elaine.*
> *How are you doing?*

I'm holding up, thanks,
Jeanette. Holding up fine.

> *I've meant to stop by,*
> *but between cattle and cougars . . .*

I gave Aunt J a quizzical look,
which she totally ignored.

> *You men hungry? We've*
> *got a lot of food here.*

Every time she got nervous,
the talk turned to food.

> *Chicken and biscuits and three*
> *kinds of salads . . .*

Definitely nervous. He had
to be *that* Kevin.

> *Not to mention pie. Pattyn*
> *helped me with the pies. . . .*

Kevin was *her* Kevin,
and Kevin was Ethan's dad.

How could she have neglected
to mention such an important thing?

I Wasn't Sure

If Ethan knew about their history,
so I sat, semi-stunned, and watched
the two of them reconnect.

As they talked, years and regret
seemed to melt away from Aunt J's
face. She was seventeen again.

Ethan's dad kept sliding closer
to Aunt J . . . or was that just
my overactive imagination?

It was kind of surreal, like a ghost
had materialized from out of Aunt J's
past, a ghost who lived right down the road.

Did they never see each other?
It seemed they hadn't, but how could
that be, with them in such close proximity?

Had Ethan's mom known about
them? Aunt J said she was a friend.
And how about Stan? Did he know?

Ethan cradled my hand and discussed
the pros and cons of the band's
raw attempts at bluegrass.

My heart beat faster, just sitting
so close to him, and the love I felt
for him made me even more confused.

How could Kevin and Aunt J spend
so many years, so near each other,
and make no effort to rekindle their love?

After Stuffing Ourselves

Ethan and I wandered
off for a little alone time.

The air had cooled a bit,
come dusk, and one by one

the stars began to fill
the darkening sky.

Ethan cinched his arm
around my waist

and as we walked, I noted
other women's envious stares.

Having never before been
an object of envy,

I wasn't sure how to react—
proud or protective.

Once or twice, really pretty
women smiled at Ethan

and that Jolly Green Monster
bit into me with razor-sharp teeth.

When we were by ourselves,
  I got the courage to say,

"You could have your choice
of pretty women. Why me?"

You're like the ocean, Pattyn.
Pretty enough on the surface,

but dive down into your depths,
  you'll find beauty most

people never see. Lucky me.
  I fell in, headfirst.

I Was Dying to Know

If Ethan had any idea about
Aunt J and his dad.
So as we watched people

dance, I casually asked,
"How long has Aunt J
known your father?"

A very long time, I
guess. He said they
met in high school.

"Did your mom go
to high school with
them too?"

No. Dad met Mom after
college, when he moved
to Caliente.

"Funny how both
he and Aunt J ended
up here," I tested.

Yeah, it is kind of a
coincidence. In fact, once
I heard my parents talking . . .

Just then a loudspeaker
interrupted, *Ladies and gents,*
the fireworks are about to begin!

Fireworks

Gold Red Silver Blue Green

sprays haze beauty rise eyes

high sky heaven stuns Ethan's

faze plays designs mind find

sight light perfect divine mine

inspire desire blessed flow reveal

releasing unceasing increasing

love

Ethan Drove Me Home

His dad rode with Aunt J,
and I wondered as we found
a place to park beneath
the moonlight just what
might transpire between
the adult members of our
interconnected families.

Did they, too, find a private
spot, unroll a quilted
sleeping bag in the bed
of the pickup? Did they talk
and kiss and ultimately
shed their clothes to lay
naked beneath a sea of stars?

For me, it was something all
new, memory in the making.
For Aunt J, it would be
recollection reborn.
For me, it was awakening.
For Aunt J, it would
be reawakening.

Of course, maybe they just
drove home, said their
good nights and nice-to-see-
you-agains, and went home
to their cold, lonely beds.
The cynic in me thought it likely.
The romantic begged to differ.

Vibrant Singing

Woke me the next morning.
Aunt J was in a very good mood.
I went downstairs without
dressing, eager to ask questions.
Poor Aunt J didn't know what hit her.

"Ethan's dad is your Kevin?
Why didn't you tell me?"

> She shrugged. *Didn't
> seem important.*

"Not important? You said
he was the love of your life."

> *"Was" being the operative
> word. We're just friends now.*

"But he moved to Caliente
for *you*, didn't he?"

> She shrugged again. *Could
> be. Didn't much matter by then.*

"Sure it did. So how could
he marry someone else?"

> *You'd have to ask him that.
> But I was married to Stan.*

"But what about after
Stan died?"

*Kevin was married to Elaine by then.
Marriage is a contract, Pattyn.*

"But didn't the two of
you ever . . . ?"

*Ever what? Fool around? You
should know me better than that.*

"I do. I'm sorry. But you
still love him, don't you?"

*Real love doesn't die, remember?
But sometimes that doesn't matter.*

Of course it mattered!
"So what about now?"

*I don't know about now, darlin'.
I can't predict the future.*

"But the two of you
are all alone. . . ."

She looked at me and grinned.
Not exactly. No, not at all.

I Wasn't Quite Ready to Quit

"Aunt J, I think you should
give each other a chance.
You looked pretty happy
together last night."

*We were happy last night.
But we're both lugging
old hurt around, and
that's hard to get past.*

I could understand
that. Forgiveness wasn't
easy. But they had to
try. "Please try."

*If it makes you feel
any better, he's taking
me to dinner Friday
night. So I guess we'll try.*

Yes! One more thing
bothered me. "I don't
think Ethan knows
about the two of you."

*Kevin might feel differently,
but I would never ask you
to keep secrets, especially
from someone you love.*

I shook my head. "I
don't want to keep
secrets from Ethan, but
I don't want to tell him."

Mostly because I didn't
want him to know
exactly how terrible
my father could be.

July Took on a Rhythm

Aunt J and I spent
weekdays warding
off the

           heat wave

and trying to keep
things watered.
The garden would

           wither

without attention
in the cool of early
morning. The

           simmer

of afternoon kept
us basking in front
of a big whirling fan.

           Hot

thoughts about Ethan
crept into my sick
little brain. I felt

           out

of my mind with
missing him when
he wasn't by my

           side.

After the sun drifted
low and bloomed rose,
he'd come rolling

           around

for evening visits,
coaxing my personal
temp well above the

           one hundred

mark, no matter
what the thermometer
happened to read.

On Weekends

We'd drive to the lake
or take the horses for
long morning rides,
always bringing
the rifles along. I
would never be
unprepared again.

Ethan taught me more
about the finer points
of marksmanship than I
would ever have
learned on my own.
I was good.
He was awesome.

Making love indeed
became an integral part
of our couplehood.
Ethan taught me a lot
about that, too, and
somehow the more I learned
the less guilt I suffered.

Kevin and Aunt J were
seeing each other
fairly regularly.
Ethan didn't talk
about that much, so
one day I asked,
"Does it bother you?"

A little, he admitted.
*Mom's only been gone
for eight months.
But I don't want him
to be lonely, and I can't
think of a better person
for him than Jeanette.*

I couldn't either.

So with Ethan's Blessing

Kevin was dating Aunt J.

     And I was dating Ethan.

They would go out on weekends.

     We saw each other whenever we could.

Sometimes we all had dinner.

     Sometimes we all saw a movie together.

Most of the time, they went their way.

     And, always, they let us go ours.

It was all too good to be true.

     It was Cinderella and Prince Charming, squared.

It was approaching happily ever after.

     It was Paradise, awaiting Armageddon.

Toward the End of the Month

A letter came from home. I tore it open
eagerly, to find this, from Jackie:

Dear Pattyn,

*I hope your summer has been wonderful. Why
haven't you written? Too busy chasing
tumbleweeds? Ha ha.*

*Chasing tumbleweeds would be better than how
things are here. Some vacation! All I do all day
is take care of the kids. I wouldn't mind so much
if I had you here to talk to. I wouldn't even
ask you to help! Well, not much, anyway.*

*Mom is due in October, and she's gained fifty
pounds already. All she does is sit, eat, watch
TV, and pack on pounds while we kids survive
on oatmeal and peanut butter.*

*You'd think Dad would be happy, what with
Samuel coming and all. But he's not. Friday
nights are worse than ever. Sometimes Dad
gets home, already half-drunk. I always hope
he'll get home totally drunk so maybe he'll*

pass out right away. You can see the anger growing inside him. Where did all that come from, anyway? And now it has nowhere to go. He can't hit Mom because of the baby.

Anyway, I miss you. Hope you come home soon.

Love you lots,
Your Favorite Sister
(aren't I?)

It Was My First Real Tinge

Of homesickness, despite the less-
than-rosy picture. I did miss Jackie,
did miss the girls, and I wondered
if they had changed as much as I.

Then I had to laugh. It had only
been two months. How much
could everyone change? Surely
not nearly as much as I.

I had discovered love, sex,
acceptance. I had found
a place where I felt like I
counted, a place I belonged.

I had come to think of myself
as not bad to look at, not
bad to be with, surely not
in league with Satan.

I had come to think of myself
as almost a woman, and
a woman of value. I had come
to think of myself as my own.

So why did I still feel such
connection with a place
that made me question my
place in the world?

Of Course, When Ethan Stopped By

That perceived connection

        severed immediately.

No thought of Carson City

        as we watched a Caliente sunset.

No thought of Jackie

        while Ethan discussed his day.

No thought of my sisters

        when he took me in his arms.

No thought of home

        as his lips mastered mine.

No thought of Mom

        with the slip of my clothing.

No thought of Dad

        to interfere with the blending

        of our bodies, the mesh of skin

        and the song of hearts in love.

August Rumbled In

Literally. The first week, each
morning segued into afternoon
with the grumble of thunder
over western hills.

The sky seethed with ozone,
leaking a scent hot and electric.
The animals scrambled
for cover at its steady approach.

Aunt J and I would sit on
the porch, watching carbonated
clouds bubble and blacken the sky
like a spill of cola.

We could use the rain, Aunt J
would say, *but dry lightning
is a monster no thirsty patch
of desert wants to meet.*

I didn't know what she meant
until the day I saw the greasy smoke,
off in the distance, signaling
sagebrush burning.

I've heard a high-rise fire
is a terrible thing, flames gulping
down buildings, one story at a time,
like a twenty-course meal.

But a brush fire is almost unconquerable.
Not enough hoses in all of Nevada
to stop a blaze fueled by drought-
drained sage and fed by a furious wind.

Took five days of 'copters and tankers
and 'dozers, working almost round
the clock, plus one day of blessed
pounding rainfall, to do that monster in.

Both Ethan and His Dad

Were volunteer firefighters.
Aunt J and I saw them only

if they happened to be there
when we delivered food
and water to the fire line.

All the men would trundle
in, faces smudged with soot,

bodies in need of rest and
spirits sagging. We did our
best to cheer them up

but smiles were in short
supply that week.

Even Ethan's unflagging
cheerfulness had dissolved
in a sea of exhaustion.

I saw him twice in five days.
Both times he said the same thing.

*I can keep going, but I need
to hear one thing and only
you can say it.*

So I did. "I love you, Ethan.
And I'm very proud of you."

The Old Pattyn

Might have seen
the events of that week
for what they were.

An omen.

The gut-wrenching stab
of separation, with Ethan
away for five days, was

a sign

of things to come.
But the improved Pattyn
couldn't intuit even

a whisper

of impending implosion.
Happiness, you see,
is just an illusion

of Fate,

a heavenly sleight of hand
designed to make you believe
in fairy tales. But there's

no happily ever after.

You'll only find happy
endings in books.
Some books.

The Rest of the Story

Began with another letter from home:

Hey,

*I shouldn't be writing this, and I can
only hope that whoever gets the mail
there isn't a busybody. I just don't know
where else to turn. Not that I expect
you to do anything. Please don't.
It would only make things worse.*

*I need someone to know what's going
on here, Pattyn. I need to believe someone
cares. If anyone does, it's you. Remember
I told you Dad doesn't hit Mom anymore,
because of the baby? Well, he hasn't
exactly quit his Friday night boxing
matches. Only now his opponent
isn't Mom. It's me.*

*Remember how we wondered why
she didn't tell anyone? Now I know.
It isn't only fear. It's embarrassment.
You can't show your face in public
without feeling like you've done*

something wrong. Something you
needed to be punished for. Not only that, but
everyone knows you've been bad.
Somehow, you've been bad.

But I haven't done anything wrong.
Haven't been bad. So why do I
feel guilty? Am I sick, or what?

Miss you, Jackie

Anger Sweated

From my pores, acid. I could
picture Jackie, going to sacrament
meeting wearing sunglasses.
Was that a lie too, Bishop Crandall?

Or maybe Dad was too smart
to leave bruises on his teenage
daughter. Maybe he planted his anger
where no one was likely to see it.

Not that anyone would look hard
enough to take notice until school
started again in September. Teachers
were trained to notice, weren't they?

But what if he really hurt her?
Jackie didn't have near the padding
Mom did. And who could she
turn to if he did? Who cared but me?

I didn't know what to do.
If I confided in Aunt J, she'd want
to do something, call someone—
Dad or the cops.

Jackie was right. If Dad
knew she had told anyone, even me,
maybe even *especially* me,
who knew what his reaction might be?

I stared out the window, shaking
with anger and frustration.
Then I crumbled and cried,
sinking in helplessness.

The Letter Ate at Me for Days

It seemed like I could do something,
should do something. But what?

> I didn't dare call the police. I had no
> solid proof and Dad would just deny it.

Besides, I no longer trusted the law,
nor those who had sworn to uphold it.

> I couldn't call Bishop Crandall. In his eyes,
> Jackie was just another of Dad's possessions.

Anyway, he probably already knew the truth
through one of Dad's sicko confessions.

> I wanted to tell Ethan. But what if he said something
> to his dad? What evil memories that would stir!

No way could I stand the idea of becoming
a wedge between Kevin and Aunt J.

> I hated my dad. Every time I thought my
> life was okay after all, pretty good, in fact;

every time I believed I had escaped the gravity
of his terrible sphere, he reached out,

    whatever the distance between us, grabbed
    hold and shook till my teeth rattled.

Between That

And starting my period,
I was half puppy, half bitch
for several days, seesawing
from tucking my tail between
my legs to howling at the moon,
the sun, and everyone close by.

Poor Ethan and Aunt J didn't
know quite what to make of me.
Aunt J had seen me mad before,
but Ethan hadn't. And I wasn't
just mad. I was furious,
with no reasonable way to vent.

Hormones and hatred do not
a manageable team make.
Anyone other than Ethan
would probably have
written me off right then
and there. He didn't.

Finally, after an over-the-top
snappish episode, he put
one hand on each of my
cheeks and asked, *What*

happened, Pattyn? Why
are you acting this way?

"Nothing much," I answered,
way too snippily. "Except I'm
swollen up like a rotten gourd,
my face is threatening to explode
with pimples, and . . . and . . . my dad
is beating my little sister."

Ethan Opened His Arms

I fell into them gratefully.
"I'm sorry, I didn't mean
to tell you all that."

> *Why are you sorry? Pattyn,*
> *we are nothing if we can't*
> *tell each other our secrets.*

I wished it were only my
secrets in need of telling.
"There's a lot more. Dad . . ."

> Ethan listened to a long
> recitation of my father's sins,
> minus the part about his own dad.

"I'm scared, Ethan. For
Jackie and my sisters.
For me. And for you."

> *Don't worry about me. I can*
> *take care of myself, and I*
> *swear I'll keep you safe.*

I knew he would do
the best he could, maybe
even offer himself up.

*I'm not sure how to help
your sisters, though. Give
me some time to think, okay?*

I Thought He'd

Run

if he knew.
Instead, he offered

help,

not that I believed
he could possibly

help.

I thought he'd

turn

his back, close his
heart, slink

away.

Instead, he promised

sanctuary.

Of course, he didn't
really know Dad, the

power

of his demons, or his
warped moral code.

Safety

was a relative term. I
was safe here, hugged by

sanity.

But even with Ethan
by my side, the

closer

I let myself get to home,
the more uncertain our

future

would become.

I Made Ethan Promise

Not to tell his dad or Aunt J.
> So now my nasty family secrets
could gnaw at him, too.

Neither of us could figure
> a way to stop my dad without
calling in the authorities.

We could call Secret Witness,
> Ethan suggested. *That way no one
would know who made the call.*

I debated that for a day or two.
> Would Dad think Jackie called?
Someone from church? Me?

What would the cops find when
> they got to our house? Signs of abuse?
Simple squalor? Nothing of importance?

What would they do if they found
> something "off"? Issue a warning?
Put the girls in foster care?

Would Dad have to go to court?
        Get counseling? Would that help
or only make him angrier still?

Too many questions, with no
        clear answers. I was more confused
than ever. And it began to show.

I Didn't Smile

I didn't talk much.
I picked at my food.

One morning, Aunt J
asked, *Feeling all right?*

I stared at the table.
"Okay, I guess."

*Everything good between
you and Ethan?*

I nodded my head.
"Everything's okay."

*Well, seems to me you're
not the Pattyn I'm used to.*

How could I deny it?
"I know."

*So will you tell me what's
wrong, please?*

I shook my head.
"I can't."

*Pattyn, you're not in
the family way, are you?*

"No! That's not it."
I almost wished it was.

At least then.

Journal Entry, August 14

Something inside me is shouting,
some instinct telling me to run,
run fast before everything falls
apart, like an old dust rag.

I don't know why I believed I
could actually find happiness
and hold on to it. Dad won't let
that happen, will he?

I should have known I couldn't
escape his ghosts. They followed me
here and waited for the perfect
moment to jump out and say boo.

God must be punishing me after
all. I truly was beginning to believe
Aunt J's theories about love
and God being one and the same.

I truly thought the love Ethan
and I share was blessed by God,
that He would forgive the physical
part because the rest was pure.

Maybe the Church was right.
Maybe I'm selfish.
Maybe I'm evil.
Maybe I'm damned.

I feel like I'm on a tightrope,
barely balancing. I know it's
a long way down and I'm
afraid I'm destined to crash.

Part of That Feeling of Dread

Came from the fact
that the new school
year was closing in.

The semester would start
in less than two weeks.
Where did that leave me?

I still hadn't heard
word one from home.
School here? There?

Torn between needing
to stay and wanting to leave,
wanting to be closer to Ethan,

how would I survive, not
seeing him for weeks, maybe
months, at a time?

Ethan quit his job, to spend
more time with me before
he had to pack up and go.

As the end of the month
drew nearer, each day
grew shorter than the last.

Time Became the Enemy

I could feel
the hours
slip away,
drift away,
rush away,
beyond our
reach forever.
I wanted to
melt, make
him drink
me down so
he would
carry me
inside him.

Though we
must have
eaten, must
have slept,
it seemed
all we did
was make
love, each
time better,
each time
sweeter,
each time
more frantic
than the last.

One of Those Times

I can't remember exactly
which day, only that it
was in the cool of morning,

Ethan rolled away
and said, *Oh my God.*

I knew instantly that
God had already closed
His ears. "What's wrong?"

*Don't panic, Pattyn,
but the condom tore.*

My parents had never
let me take sex ed, but
panic seemed appropriate.

*I mean, the odds are long
that anything will go wrong.*

Everything was going
wrong lately. Why should
this be any different?

*This happened to me once
before. Turned out fine.*

I didn't want to hear details.
I didn't want to consider odds.
I didn't know what to say.

*Pattyn? Are you okay?
Say something.*

"Maybe I'd better go clean up." It wasn't much, but it was all I could think to do.

One More Thing

To fret about,
in my bed at night.
Just add it to the list,
growing longer
by the minute.

I tried not to stress
too much over it.
After all, with so
many tangibles
socking my gut,

a "might be, but
probably nothing
to worry about"
didn't exactly
top my list.

And the phone call
that came a day or
two after pushed
everything else to
the back of my mind.

Aunt J Summoned Me Inside

And her eyes told me all
I needed to know.
That was your father.
He wants you home.

I'd expected it. Hoped
for it. Dreaded it. So why
did I feel so surprised?
Why did I let myself cry?

Don't do that, Pattyn.
You know I don't want
to see you go. If you cry,
I will too.

I coughed back a sob.
"But what about you?
I don't want to leave
you all by yourself."

I've been by myself for
years. Besides, thanks
mostly to you, I've got
Kevin in my life again.

The thought comforted me
a little. "But what about
Ethan? What if they won't
let me see him?"

Love is stubborn. You
two will find a way
to each other. But please
be smart about it.

She knew, as I did,
exactly what was at stake.
So I felt safe admitting,
"I'm scared, Aunt J."

You just have to make
it through this year. Then
leave. You always have
a second home. Here.

That Same Day

Another letter arrived
from Jackie, too late
to serve as a warning:

Dear Pattyn,

*I heard Mom and Dad
talking. They want you
to come home so you can
help take care of the baby.
I guess you've got enough
credits to graduate only
going to school half days.*

*I thought I'd be happier,
having you home. But I
changed my mind. If you're
okay there, and you can
find a way to stay,
don't come home, Pattyn.*

*Because then Dad
wouldn't just hit me.
He'd hit you, too.*

Love, Jackie

Dad Wanted to Come Get Me

The Saturday before school started,
although he wasn't particularly
anxious to make that long trip again.

So when Aunt J mentioned
a friend of hers was driving to Reno,
he felt more than willing to
give me permission to ride along.

Luckily, he had no clue
that person was the man I had
fallen desperately in love with.

The night before we left,
Aunt J and Kevin fixed a big
dinner, and when I came downstairs,
there were gifts on the table.

First I opened Kevin's, a book
on horsemanship, so I could
"practice up for next summer."

Aunt J handed me a small package.
Inside was a cell phone. *You can
call me anytime. Don't worry about
minutes. I've got them covered.*

Face red, but brave in spite of it,
Ethan offered an even smaller box.
My hands shook as I opened it.

Set in a gold promise ring, three
small diamonds glittered. *One
for you, one for me, one for us,*
he said sweetly. *I love you.*

Aunt J started to cry.
"You said not to do that," I scolded,
eyes tearing up too.

Kevin grinned. *Women! You
gotta love 'em. Now how
about dinner? I like my steak rare.
What about you?*

Our Last Night Together

Defined bittersweet.

It was beautiful,
laden with stars
and the serenade
of crickets, barn
owls, and bullfrogs,
late summer voices.

It was sorrowful,
filled with frail
promises that our
bloom into family
would not wither
with time, distance.

It was spectacular,
a vision of love
perfected, two
humans joined in
earthly lust and
spiritual passion.

It was the worst
night of my life,
because no matter
how hard I tried
to believe it would
all work out in the end . : .

The Old Pattyn Resurfaced

To tell the new
Pattyn she was

            crazy.

Whoever directed
her heavenly

            soul

to be placed in this
earthly body had

            suffering

in mind. Just my
luck, my

            angel

mentor was tilted
a bit to the

            sadistic

side. But why
punish an

            innocent,

unless in the end
everyone was

            guilty

of unredeemable sin,
programmed by some

sibling,

or so the Mormon
Church claimed,

of God above?

I Thought I Knew "Sad"

But saying good-bye to Aunt J
was like stepping into quicksand,
knowing it was there.

> *Whatever happens, she said,*
> *I want you to know that you*
> *have given my life back to me.*
> *It was a gift I never believed*
> *possible, and I thank you,*
> *from the depths of my heart.*
>
> *But more importantly, you*
> *are a gift, to all who know*
> *you, whether or not they realize*
> *it. If they don't, they are blind.*
> *You have a special place in this*
> *world. All you have to do is find it.*
>
> *Do not give up on yourself, on*
> *the truths you have realized.*
> *Do not give in to those who*
> *would crush your dreams like*
> *nutshells. And never turn*
> *away from forever love.*

Climbing into Ethan's truck,
driving away and back toward
Carson City, was sorrow, defined.

We Made the Long Drive

Even longer, stopping
several times along the way

to stretch our legs, enjoy
the scenery and each other.

At lunchtime, we pulled
off into a stand of trees.

Ethan reached down under
the seat and extracted

a sizeable cardboard box.
You hide this, he said, *somewhere*

your dad will never look. This
is your trump card.

Inside the box was a pistol—
a 10mm semiautomatic.

It's accurate as hell. But
you need to practice now,

and promise me you'll stay sharp.
He spent the next half hour

helping me master control
of the FBI's favorite handgun.

I wasn't sure where I could
hide it, but I was damn well

going to find a place. Armed
with a gun like that, I felt safe,

at least as safe as I was likely
to feel under my father's roof.

About Fifteen Minutes

Away from home, we
stopped for a private

good-bye.

And I tasted in our last
barrage of delectable

kisses

a growing sense of dread.
And I felt in our final

embraces

a strong premonition
not to let him go.

Promises

to stay in touch via cell
phone helped a little.

Vows

to visit when he could
helped not at all.

Tears

puddled, spilled, soaked
Ethan's shirt like

a salty stream,

fed by a downpour of despair,
roiling into a river

of mourning.

He Dropped Me Off

Early evening, just past
suppertime. Inside, we could
hear the après-dinner commotion,
and it almost felt like a welcome home.
Which was good, because I got no real
welcome home, other than the girls squealing
hello; Mom glancing up from the TV to say hi;
and Dad and Johnnie, singing together out back.

I was glad Dad didn't see
Ethan. But Mom and the girls
did when he carried my bags to
the door. Mom thought to ask who
he was and I gave a generic answer,
which she accepted without comment.
Jackie, of course, knew better. She waited
for the scoop until later that night. Whisper time.

Meanwhile, I walked
through the door with my
backpack full of books and two
suitcases, one filled with homemade
clothes. The other carried a new cell
and a new gun, tucked well inside a new
set of clothes and beneath a new quilt, which
Aunt J sent with me. No longer the new Pattyn.

I knew that as soon
as Dad stumbled into
the kitchen. *Well, look
who's home. Get me a bowl
of ice cream.* With that, he let
me know from the get-go that life in
the Von Stratten house hadn't changed
one bit. And if I somehow thought *I* had,
well, I was most definitely mistaken.

I Got Dad His Ice Cream

Without comment, mostly
because I didn't want to take
a chance on a boxing match.

     Maybe it was the L-tryptophan,
     or maybe it was just Johnnie,
     but Dad fell asleep early.

          Mom stood and made her way
          to bed. She had definitely gained
          a lot more than an eight-pound baby.

               It didn't seem the girls
               had grown so much. Not
               as much as I had, anyway.

          They were a lot easier to put
          to bed, though. Maybe they didn't
          want to chance Dad's wrath either.

Jackie and I waited until
the house was dead asleep
before filling each other in.

By then, I was so grateful
for the silence that I really
didn't want to talk. But I did.

We Both Held Back a Little

I talked about riding
horses, herding cattle,
driving pickups.

    She talked about camp—
    swimming, arts and crafts,
    LDS propaganda.

I told her I didn't go
to one sacrament
meeting all summer.

    She told me they went
    every week, despite Mom's
    morning sickness.

I talked about Aunt J,
confessed her sordid
secrets about our father.

    Which opened the door
    to Jackie's own confession
    about Dad's cruelty.

I listened to her outline
his face slaps, hair yanks,
and punches that bruised.

    She didn't tell me then
    the worst of it—a belt beating
    that made the welts bleed.

I admitted almost everything
about Ethan, omitting only
the part about making love.

         Jackie looked at my locket,
         my promise ring, and though she
         must have suspected the rest of it . . .

She Respected That Secret

Never even asked the question
that had to have been on her mind.

Just like I respected her unfinished
tale, though I knew there was more.

Some confidences require the right
moment, even between favorite sisters.

We talked late into the night
and it almost felt good being home,

sharing a bed with someone I cared
about, and who cared about me,

someone I could gush to about Ethan,
someone eager to hear

that forever love wasn't just
an invention of romance authors

and fairy tales, but something vital
and viable. Something to trust in

and hold on to when the screaming
started and the blows fell.

For Everyone Else

It was just like I'd never left,
just like there had never
been another Pattyn but the one
they'd chased away.

The next morning, we ate
breakfast, went to sacrament
meeting. No one at church
acted like I'd even been gone.

Bishop Crandall did offer
an inquisitive stare, trying to assess
the success—or failure—of my
summer punishment.

I tried not to look smug, to avoid
future problems, but it wasn't
easy, especially half listening
to bogus testimonies.

Why hadn't I noticed it before—
how everyone said virtually
the same thing and no one seemed blown
away by the meaning of their words?

I mean, if God actually tapped me on the shoulder and whispered truths into my ear, I'd definitely be impressed! And I'd show it.

And Then School Started

My senior year. I should
have been excited, but it
just seemed lame.
Trigonometry.
Astronomy.
Government.
I needed them
to graduate, but
after that, what
for? I took creative
  writing for English
    and for my elective,
      Intro to Aviation, just
        in case I ever needed to
          fly an airplane. (Right
            after I bought my first
              Ferrari!) I did need a
                PE credit too. Lucky
                  me, they counted the
                    shooting club. But all
                      the rest—dances, pep
                      rallies, football games—
                      meant nothing. And,
                      with the exception of
                      Jackie, not one of my

schoolmates meant
a damn thing either.
I wasn't one of them,
not that I'd ever *really*
felt like I was. But now
I felt miles removed.
Miles above. And I
liked it up there.

For One Thing

Up there, it was easy to look
down on Derek and Carmen.

In fact, it wasn't hard to look
down on Justin and Tiffany.

As for Becca and Emily and
the rest of my seminary crowd,

well, they'd always been
relatively worthless, anyway.

I did buddy up with Trevor,
a total germ whom I'd known

since fifth grade, completely
because he had a car—a beater,

but who cared? At least I had
a ride that wasn't Mom or Dad.

I could tell that Trevor liked
me, and I played that to the max.

He was a good Mormon boy,
meaning goofy, churchgoing,

and soon in the market
for a good Mormon wife.

He was just the kind of guy
my parents would approve of.

I Tried to Talk to Ethan

Every day, usually at lunch.
Just hearing his voice
made everything all right.
His classes were hard,
he said, but not nearly as hard
as not having me close.

For me, forever love
was only strengthened
by distance. The weird thing
was, only months before,
I had thought this kind of love
was something to veer
wide around. But I
wasn't afraid anymore.

Ethan was the first thing
on my mind every morning.
He was the last thing
I thought of, drifting off.
I couldn't wait to see him,
fall into his kisses,
fold into his body.

Every atom
of me missed him.

The First Couple of Weeks

Things weren't so bad.
At school, I tried to project the new Pattyn.
Attractive. Desirable.

That did come in handy
the first time I turned a corner and ran into
Carmen and Derek.

I flashed a cool smile,
put my nose in the air, and strode right by.
Here's the good part.

As I wiggled off in new
form-fitting jeans, I heard Carmen hiss,
Are you checking her out?

I only wished they knew
where the self-confidence had come from,
who had given me my smile.

Wouldn't Carmen take
a second look at Derek? Wouldn't Tiffany turn
chartreuse with jealousy?

I bet even Ms. Rose
would gawk and run home to her spicy novels.
And Ethan belonged to me.

# At Home

I reverted to the old Pattyn,
the one unlikely to draw much
attention to herself. Although
Mom was driving me crazy.

> (*Pattyn, please go check on*
> *the girls. Pattyn, would you vacuum?*
> *Pattyn, start the veggies—*
> like she was eating them!)

I tried to stay patient with
the girls. But for three of us,
hormones were an issue.
The others bickered constantly.

> (*I had that first.* "Did not."
> *You give it back.* "I won't."
> *I'll tell Mom and she'll tell Dad—*
> that last one often worked.)

Dad was getting ready to go
hunting. Lucky him, he got
a deer tag. Tell the truth, he was
as relaxed as I'd ever seen him.

> (*Gonna fill up that freezer*
> *with venison, long as I can get*
> *far enough up in those hills—*
> meaning pray we don't get early snow.)

Privately, I thought venison
was secondary. He missed
killing, and now he'd have
a chance to scratch that itch.

But Then Things Got Tough at Work

A big gathering of Yucca Mountain protesters
was expected at the capitol the following
week, when Department of Energy
representatives met with the governor.

> That Friday evening Dad hit Johnnie
> early, trying to dull the edge. *Goddamn
> protesters. Reminds me of the seventies.
> Who do those shitheads think they are?*

I can't believe I said a word, dared
to express an opinion. "It's called
free speech, Dad. It's guaranteed
in the Constitution, you know."

> Dinner table babble fizzled as Dad
> put down his fork. *No one has a right
> to question the government, missy.
> Especially not those liberal loudmouths.*

Damn the new Pattyn! She flat
wouldn't take the hint. "Do you know
how many tons of radioactive crap
will move through Carson City?"

"Crap" was Aunt J's term for it. Dad
was suitably impressed. *Did I hear you
say "crap"? What kind of word is that for
a daughter of mine to use?*

I should have stopped. I didn't.
"Crap is exactly what it is, Dad.
Tons and tons of poisonous poop,
traveling right down Highway 395."

Dad pushed back from the dinner table,
jumped to his feet. *I will not tolerate
that language from you. You will respect
me and all the things I stand for. . . .*

I really don't know what got into
me, but I brought my eyes level with
his and said, "Not if one of the things
you stand for is Yucca Mountain."

Dumb Idea, Oh Yeah

In one very quick movement,
he came around the table,
grabbed my hair, pulled
me out of the chair, tossed
me to my knees on the floor.

>   I could hear the girls scramble,
>   suffered a hot wind of Johnnie WB.
>   *You little bitch. You live in my*
>   *house. Eat my food. I'm not*
>   *putting up with your shit anymore.*

He pushed my head against
the floor and my face scraped
dirty linoleum. That was the
best of it. Because then his fist
began to hail against my back.

>   *You will remember who I am.*
>   *You will remember who I am . . .*
>   *remember who I am.*
>   His mantra fell, rhythmic
>   accompaniment for his drumming.

Finally, he tired, or he could
no longer resist Johnnie's call.
I just lay there, afraid
to move, hoping he'd
missed everything vital.

Journal Entry, Sep 15

Okay, I was really stupid.
Spouted off to Dad.
And boy did he give me a major
reminder about manners
at the dinner table.

I'm lying here on my stomach
because my back feels mushy
and I know it must be a mess.
It doesn't really hurt, thanks
to the eight aspirin I took.
That's probably enough
to kill me. Wonder if
aspirin dulls the pain
of its killing you.

Jackie helped me to bed, iced
the worst of the bruises.
Mom just sat glued to
reality TV, like it could
be half as good
as the very real show
in the kitchen tonight.

I'm trying hard to despise
Dad for what he did to me.
But part of me thinks I deserved
it. Besides, compared to other
episodes in the Stephen
Von Stratten saga,
this chapter
was nothing.

Dad Took Off Hunting

In the dark of the next morning.
I heard him go. Once the aspirin
wore off, I didn't get much sleep.

It sort of surprised me that he'd
head off into the hills, with
Mom so close to her due date.

But Mom insisted she wasn't
ready to go into labor yet.
And I guessed she should know.

At least I didn't have to look
at Dad, make him breakfast,
bring him ice cream.

In the afternoon Jackie took
the girls outside to play while
Mom indulged in a nap.

I used the time to sneak
a call to Ethan and tell
him what had happened.

I got his voice mail, so
didn't admit more than
how very much I loved him.

Then I called Aunt J, not to
detail my destruction, but to hear
the voice of someone who cared.

Easy Enough

Come Sunday
to find things to
despise, starting with
Bishop Crandall, sitting up
front, defining at least three
of my favorite swear words. He
should want to help me, help any
woman condemned to a man's fist.

I looked at Sister Crandall, all gray
and wrinkled like a rhinoceros, and
I wondered if she had ever had to
come to church propped up by
a half-dozen aspirin. Other
women passed my seat.
I assessed each,
seeking signs.

This building,
disguised as a house
of worship, was rather like
a hive. A backward hive, for
honeybees, at least, have the good
sense to worship the female that gifts
them all with life. They do not hold
their drones in such high esteem. But

here, in this hive of hornets, the males
flitted flower to flower, pollinating and
stinging and injecting their poison. I
hated everything this place stood
for, except the one thing it
claimed—and miserably
failed—to represent:
my Heavenly father.

My Earthly Father

Returned from his trip very
late that Sunday night.

He pulled Jackie and me
out of bed to help him

unload a five-point buck
from the top of the Subaru.

Gutted but not skinned,
the deer from behind

looked merely asleep.
But when we came around

in front, death was everywhere—
in the thick

crimson ropes and spatters
on the hood, windows, and doors;

in the repulsive perfume leaking
from the animal's gaping belly;

and in its frigid stare. Oh, most
definitely, death was rampant there.

I staggered a few steps away
from the car and vomited foreboding.

By the Time I Got Up

For school the next day,
the buck had been neatly
butchered, wrapped, and
stacked into freezer-size
packages. The hide, head,
and other detritus were
bagged and left for the trash
man. Dad's speed and skill
with a butcher knife were
straight out of a novel:
The Silence of the Fawns.

        Just another reminder to
        keep my mouth shut about
        Friday night. I sat in class,
        pulsing pain as my muscles
        struggled to heal themselves.
        Around me the everyday
        sounds of classrooms and
        hallways—laughter, locker
        doors, feet skids on polished
        wood—echoed. It was all
        so normal, all so right. And
        I could relate to none of it.

In the past I'd always
felt possessed. Neglected.
Unloved. School had offered
escape from home's daily
suffocation. But now I felt
marked. Branded. Abused.
Those scars would follow
me there from home. School
would never again gift me
with haven. It became just
another chore, something
to get over with. Very soon.

Dad Fired the Next Volley

Three weeks later.
It was only Thursday,
but Johnnie accompanied him
through the kitchen door,
up the hall, and into the bathroom.

The two of them found
a flood of toilet water.
A plunger revealed
the culprit—a sanitary
napkin, become quite
unsanitary by that time.

It belonged to 'Lyssa,
just past thirteen and
never instructed in correct
disposal methods. But
it could have been
Jackie's. Or mine.

Dad called all three of us
into the hallway. *Which one
of you did this?* Spit
dribbled from his mouth
and his red eyes were
rimmed with anger.

And when I dared look
up into them, I found
the hunger of the cougar.
'Lyssa crumbled. But
before she could own up,
I lied. "I did. I'm sorry."

The Cougar Pounced

And this time I had no
Ethan to save me from his

lethal

claws, shoot him down,
dead and harmless. A

vicious

paw struck the side of
my face. The nasty

slash

tore a pierced earring from
its lobe. A second blow

caught

the other ear, smack where
sounds went in. It made

me

reel, but I managed to keep
my feet, despite the clanging.

At the

moment I lifted defensive
arms, Dad caught my

throat,

held tight, applied pressure.
And as his calloused hands

closed tight,

I barely heard his snarl,
betraying absolutely

no pity:

*You don't know what sorry
is, little girl. But you will.*

When He Was Finished

The only thing I was sorry
about was coming home
in the first place.

I could barely hear,
through the throbbing
quicksand in my ears.

I could barely swallow
through the puffing finger
marks around my neck.

I could barely taste,
beyond the bulging
of my tongue,

the coppery flavor
of blood, crusting
my gums.

But I wasn't sorry
I stepped forward.
'Lyssa might have died.

And as I crawled off to bed,
a couple of very important
things forded my soupy mind.

The first was how much easier
it was to hate my dad that night.
I'd said nothing but "sorry."

The second was, flushed or not,
the Kotex probably should
have been mine.

August . . . August . . . ?
It had been almost seven
weeks since my last period.

Jackie Tried to Comfort Me

In bed that night,
but all I could do was cry.
And I couldn't even tell
her the real reason why.
I couldn't be pregnant,
could I?

(Could!)

If I was, what would
I do?

(Would it even
be up to me to decide?)

Would Ethan do the right
thing?

(Was getting married
the right thing?)

Even if he would, would
Mom and Dad let me?

(Would they rather have
me a single mother?)

Even if they'd let me,
is that what I wanted?

(Considering my whole
take on marriage and kids?)

If I did want to and they
said no, what then?

Was I pregnant?

(Could we sneak off
somewhere and do it?)

(Of course I was.)

Would Ethan marry me?

(Of course he would.)

Was there a way around
Mom and Dad?

(Of course there was.)

So was that what I wanted?

(???)

I Couldn't Go to School

The next day
(I looked like I'd crawled
off a battlefield),
so I had plenty
of time to think about it.
The more I did, the sicker
I became. Just my luck,
one reject condom
and the end of my life—
one way or another—
was well within sight.

And then, out of nowhere,
Mom's water broke.
She made a hasty phone call
to Dad, but he was busy
with a bomb threat
and couldn't get away.
After seven babies, this
one was destined to come
fast. Mom's contractions
were immediately strong
and close together. She
started to panic, when I
volunteered, "I'll drive you."

As Mom grabbed her bag,
I loaded Georgia into her car seat,
then climbed behind the steering
wheel. Mom did think to ask if
I really knew how to drive, so
on the way to the hospital,
I told her the whole story.
Why not? At that point I had
nothing much to lose.
When we arrived, she asked
me not to go inside, using some
excuse about not wanting
Georgia there, and the girls needing
someone to come home to.

But the real reason was obvious.
At hospitals, people ask questions
about kids with swollen faces.

Driving Home

I thought how easy it would be
to just keep on going.

Except   I had Georgia.

Except   I had no money
and the van was riding near empty.

Except   it would change
nothing. I still had decisions
to make if my fears proved correct.

Except   I needed to talk
to Ethan before I made any
decisions. And I couldn't tell him
I was pregnant until I knew for sure.

Except   I really, really
needed to talk to him right
that very minute before I went
completely crazy about The Way
Things Were—incomprehensible.

Now Dad Believed

A good Mormon woman
should have to ask her husband
for money. Even grocery money
was supposed to be a joint decision.

But Mom had a secret cash stash,
funded by singles and small change,
"borrowed" from Dad's pockets
when he and Johnnie passed out.

Like everything in her life, her cash
jar was chaotic. I was pretty sure she
had no real idea just how much money
was inside. So I swiped a few dollars.

Georgia and I took a little ride to the store—
and not our usual grocery store, but one
where everyone looked like strangers.
There I purchased an Early Pregnancy Test.

Good thing Georgia couldn't read yet,
and to keep her from asking too many
questions, I bought her a lollipop
and a carton of milk for the refrigerator.

We made it home just minutes before
the first of three school buses dropped
off a brood of Von Stratten girls.
I put them straight on their homework.

Then I went into the bathroom,
carefully followed the directions,
and within a few minutes I had
my answer, in a little blue line.

Pounding on the Door

Brought me out of my semicatatonic
state. I scrambled to hide the evidence
so Roberta could come in and pee.

On the way past the mirror, I caught
sight of a face and had to do a double
take. Could that battered hag be me?

I looked just like my mom, give
or take maybe ninety pounds.
Was that who I'd be in a few years?

I had only one person to turn to . . .
okay, maybe two. Aunt J would never
turn me away. But I needed Ethan.

I went into my bedroom and removed
the bottom drawer of my dresser,
revealing the hollow underneath.

I had discovered the place quite
by accident—no one but me ever
moved a dresser to vacuum!

This was my personal secret hiding
place, and as I reached for the cell,
my hand brushed something

cool and hard and instantly
comforting—the 10mm. Waiting . . .
Just then the front door slammed.

Dad!

Journal Entry, Oct 7

One of my worst nightmares
has come true. I'm pregnant.
I really don't know what to do.
I can't even call Ethan until
Monday. Ethan. God, I need
him so much.

It's kind of weird, because
as scared as I am, a part of me
is really happy to have Ethan's
baby growing inside me.
A little Ethan, tucked right there.
I need something beautiful inside,
because outside I'm so ugly right now.

Mom brought baby Sam home
today. Oops . . . Samuel. No need
to stir Dad's pot. I'm just starting
to heal from the last time.
Anyway, Samuel's all red and scrunched
up and not pretty at all.
Will my baby look like that?
I don't think so.

My baby will be perfect because he's part Ethan, part me. He? Where did that come from?

On Monday

I didn't look so bad, so Dad
let me go to school,
with one heartfelt warning,

Family secrets stay
behind these doors.

Like I didn't know that.
But I simply nodded
and kept my mouth shut.

Come straight home.
Your mother needs help.

Like I wouldn't come
straight home. Like I didn't
know she needed help.

I want the house picked
up. Groceries put away.

He'd bought them the day
before. The canned goods
still sat in bags on the floor.

Keep the youngsters
out of your mom's hair.

Yadda. Yadda. She needed
her rest. Poor Mom. Having
a baby sure took it out of her.

*You do remember how
to change a diaper, don't you?*

Every answer I came up
with would have gotten me
into trouble. So I just smiled.

By Lunch My Fingernails Were History

I got hold of Ethan on the first ring.
    He asked me where I'd been since Thursday.

I tried to think where to begin. . . .
    He asked if everything was okay.

I told him no, choked on my words. . . .
    He said to tell him the whole thing, he had all day.

I started with the Kotex episode. : . .
    He kept completely quiet as I outlined my injuries.

I moved on to driving Mom to the hospital. . . .
    He didn't say a word as I segued into the drive to the store.

I broke down into quiet tears. . . .
    He begged me not to cry, to finish my story.

I confessed that I was pregnant.
    He promised it wasn't the end of the world.

I whispered that I was scared.
        He said not to worry, it would all be okay.

I might have believed him,
        had I not glanced behind me right then.

Carmen and Tiffany

Had heard the whole thing, or at least
enough of it to know my predicament.

Oh God, the gleeful look on their faces.
Now they possessed a powerful weapon.

If you've never been on the wrong end
of gossip, spread by malicious girls,

you'd be surprised how fast they can
disseminate reputation-crushing information.

By the next day, practically everyone in school knew.
I could see it in their eyes, hear it in their laughter.

Even Jackie found out through the grapevine.
She came to me, asked if it was true.

What could I do but admit everything?
When she asked what I was going to do,

I still didn't have an answer. But when
I called Ethan again, he had one.

Marry me, Pattyn. You know I love you. I'll love the baby, too.

And I'll love and take care of both of you until the day I die.

He Wanted Me to Tell

Mom and Dad, but when
I considered what happened
over a flushed Kotex, I couldn't do it.

> *We can't get married*
> *without their permission.*

"Then we'll wait until I'm eighteen.
The baby won't care. Please,
Ethan. Come and get me."

> I was asking him to kidnap me.
> *Pattyn, I don't know . . .*

"Ethan, if my dad finds out, he's
liable to kill me. Or you. Let me
tell you a story. . . ."

> He listened to an ugly recitation
> about my dad, his dad, and Aunt J.

"I didn't want to tell you, but you
have to understand what kind
of man we're dealing with."

> He promised to come pick me up
> from school on Thursday.

"Why Thursday?" I wasn't
sure it could wait another day.
"Why not tomorrow?"

I can't bring you back to the dorm.
I have to find a place for us to stay.

That Night I Prayed

Harder than I'd ever
prayed before.

"Please, God, give us the chance
to be a family. The right kind of family."

In answer, overnight, He delivered
an Arctic Event. A freezing cold

air mass moved in from the north,
bringing early snow to the mountains.

Down below we got sleet, which
froze overnight into oceans of black ice.

The temperature hovered just a bit over
twenty degrees. Winter, in October.

Meanwhile, word continued to spread.
When Trevor picked me up that day,

I knew he'd heard. He clamped his
hands on the steering wheel as his

old Chevy fishtailed on the ice.
"Careful, Trevor," I urged.

You mean careful like you weren't? he jeered.

I Knew He Was Hurt

So I pretended ignorance.
> But ignorance, real or imagined,
>> could not halt the ugly rumor mill.

It was déjà vu all over again.
> Trevor told Becca and Emily.
>> Becca couldn't wait to tell her mom.

Her mom went straight to
> Sister Rhinoceros Crandall, who
>> shared the good news with her husband.

That evening my mom got
> a call. I saw her face turn paper
>> white and knew it was all coming down.

But instead of telling Dad
> right then, she called me into
>> her room. *Tell me it isn't true.*

One day. I only had to
> punt for one day. So I said,
>> "Tell you what isn't true?"

She really didn't want
        that kind of trouble. *Pattyn,*
                tell me you aren't pregnant.

I mustered up a look
        of sheer disbelief. "Why would
                you even ask such a thing?"

She bought the whole
        package. I had punted eighty
                yards. But it wasn't quite enough.

Somehow I Made It

Through the next day, and when
I saw Ethan's Dodge turn
into the parking lot, I ran,
almost slipping on the ice.

I flew through the door,
into his arms, and the warmth
of his kisses. As we drove
off, I noticed Trevor

standing there, watching.
What I didn't see was him
taking down Ethan's license
plate number.

Rather than waste time driving
to Reno to reach the interstate,
Ethan chose the more treacherous
route over the mountain, into California.

The highway had been plowed,
but not well, and even in four-wheel
drive, the tires spun a bit on the steeper
stretches of icy pavement.

Suddenly, Ethan said, *Oh shit*.
I turned to see red and blue lights
coming up quickly behind us.
"Don't stop!" I commanded.

Instead, Ethan picked up speed,
a bad thing to do in those
conditions. My heart raced as
we went sideways around a curve.

Ethan corrected, the Dakota
skidded sideways. He turned
into the skid, but too hard.
Hold on! he shouted.

It Was the Last Thing

I ever heard him say.
I floated up into a cloud of white.

Were we in California?

"Ethan?" I heard myself ask.
Movement. *She's awake,* someone said.

Pattyn? Can you hear me?

Did they think I was deaf?

"Where am I?"

Barton Memorial. You were in an accident.

Accident? The Dakota . . . "Where's Ethan?"

Silence. Way too much silence.

Where were the faces that went with the voices?

There. I screamed at them. "Where is Ethan?"

I'm sorry, honey, said a nurse. *He didn't make it.*

Didn't make it? They couldn't mean . . .

"No! He's not dead! He can't be dead! I won't let him be dead!

Oh God, not dead!"

But He Was

And so was the baby.

Dead.

Even that precious
piece of Ethan.

Dead.

All because of Trevor.

Dead.

Trevor, who called
my mom.

Dead.

Mom, who called Dad.

Dead.

Dad, who called his buddy
the highway patrolman.

Dead.

Everything I loved.

Dead.

Everything I had to
live for.

Dead.

Why couldn't I be

dead

too? It was the least
God could have done.

I Was in the Hospital

For over a week.
They said my head
had to heal.
I knew it never would,
not inside.

Mom and Dad
didn't visit me once.
Dad had to work.
Mom had a new baby
to take care of.

Bishop Crandall
came by. He said with prayer
and perseverance,
God might one day
forgive me.

Might.
One day forgive me.
I didn't want
His forgiveness.
I wanted Him to let me die.

But He wouldn't
even do that. No, He
wanted to punish
me for loving Ethan.
Forever.

Aunt J was wrong.
God wasn't love, couldn't
be love.
Because for me,
love was a corpse.

When I Finally

Did come home, no
one was allowed to speak
to me. Dad had officially
disowned me.

He wanted me out.
But I had no place to go.
Aunt J's was not
an option. I could never look
Kevin in the eye again.

I only hoped
he wouldn't blame Aunt J
for the sins of her niece.
His only son's death
was all my fault.

The two of them needed
each other more than ever,
needed their own forever
love to quell the pain
of such loss.

Jackie tried
to intercede on my behalf,
but Dad wouldn't
listen, and Mom knew better
than to say a word.

Dad had a new
son. He didn't need
just one more daughter,
especially not one
as obnoxious as I.

And so, with
nothing at all to lose,
and not much
to gain but revenge, I began
to form my plan.

See, as Far as I'm Concerned

My life is over.
My one forever love has
been snatched away,
condemned by my own
father's rules to die,
just because he loved me.

I am without a home,
without a single person to love.
And after having
discovered love, lived for a short
while surrounded by love,
that is too much to bear.

I am a pariah, at church,
at school. The few people
I once called friends have
betrayed me and caused
the death of my husband,
our innocent child.

And so they should die too.
All of them. Dad. Bishop
Crandall. Trevor, Becca, Emily.
With the pull of a 10mm hair

trigger, their lives will end
at sacrament meeting.
Such lovely irony!

And when I finish there,
I'll hide in the desert,
reload, and go in search
of Carmen and Tiffany,
who started the rumors.
And Derek, just because.

Plans Made

I am sitting on the hard cement
railing of a freeway overpass.

Legs dangling,
I watch the unrelenting motion
of normal people in daily transit.

Mind-boggling,
how so many separate lives travel
in such remarkable unison.

Soul searching,
I know that I will never squeeze
into such a common mold.

Brain racing,
I struggle to reach a decision.
God, whoever He is, only knows which way I'll go.

Heart breaking,
I think that if Dad, staring down the sight of a 10mm,
would only tell me he loves me,

I could easily change my mind . . .

. . . but he won't.

Author's Note

This book is fiction, but much in it is true—in particular, the stories about nuclear issues in Nevada. Those "downwinders" still alive—and their children—suffer health problems directly related to the aboveground nuclear testing that took place at the Nevada Test Site in the middle part of the twentieth century. People really were encouraged to have "blast parties," or otherwise to sit outside to watch the mushroom clouds. The radiation badges they wore were later collected to gather data about radiation levels. I didn't want this information to die along with the remaining downwinders.

Parts of Nevada are desert. It is also the most mountainous state in the country, and there are beautiful rivers, lakes, and forests. It is much more than "sand and sagebrush"—not a wasteland at all. Pattyn, the protagonist in this book, comes to love rural Nevada, where the spirit of the Old West lives on in its people. It is my hope that the portrait I paint of this rugged land will help you come to love it too.

Raeanne Mirror, Mirror

When I look into a
mirror,
it is her face I see.
Her right is my left, double
moles, dimple and all.
My right is her left,
unblemished.

We are exact
opposites,
Kaeleigh and me.
Mirror-image identical
twins. One egg, one sperm,
one zygote, divided,
sharing one complete
set of genetic markers.

On the outside
we are the same. But not
inside. I think
she is the egg, so
much like our mother
it makes me want to scream.

Cold.
Controlled.
        That makes me the sperm,
        I guess. I take completely
        after our father.
        All Daddy, that's me.
Codependent.
Cowardly.

        Good, bad. Left, right.
        Kaeleigh and Raeanne.
        One egg, one sperm.
        One being, split in two.

        And how many
souls?

Interesting Question

Don't you think?
I mean, if the Supreme
Being inserts a single soul
at the moment of conception,
does that essence divide
itself? Does each half then
strive to become again
whole, like a starfish
or an earthworm?

Or might the soul clone itself,
create a perfect imitation
of something yet to be
defined? In this way,
can a reflection be altered?

Or does the Maker,
in fact, choose
to place two
separate souls within
a single cell, spark
the skirmish that ultimately
causes such an unlikely rift?

Do twins begin in the womb?
Or in a better place?

About the Author

Ellen Hopkins has been writing poetry for years and has also published several nonfiction books. Her first novel, *Crank*, released in 2004 and quickly became a word-of-mouth sensation, garnering praise from teens and critics alike. Ellen's other novels include *Impulse* and *Glass*, the sequel to *Crank*. She lives with her husband and son in Carson City, Nevada. Visit www.ellenhopkins.com and www.myspace.com/ellenhopkins.

FIND YOUR EDGE WITH THESE STARTLING AND
STRIKING BOOKS—ALL FROM FIRST-TIME NOVELISTS.

JASON MYERS

AMANDA MARRONE

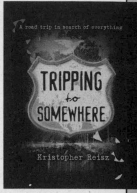

KRISTOPHER REISZ

Gritty. Electrifying. Real.

ALLISON VAN DIEPEN

KRISTEN TRACY

THE BESTSELLING STORY OF ONE BOY'S DESCENT INTO DRUGS AND HIS EVENTUAL RESURRECTION

nic sheff **TWEAK**

[Growing up on methamphetamines]

From Atheneum
Published by Simon & Schuster